Soar

the empire chronicles

Alyssa Rose Ivy

Cover Design: Phatpuppy Art
Cover Model Photography: K. Keeton Designs
Models: Cameo Hopper and Justin Schrock
Background Photography: Stuart Monk Photography
Formatting: Polgarus Studio

Other Books by Alyssa Rose Ivy

Flight (The Crescent Chronicles #1)
Focus (The Crescent Chronicles #2)
Found (The Crescent Chronicles #3)
The Hazards of Skinny Dipping
Derailed (Clayton Falls)
Veer (Clayton Falls)
Wrecked (Clayton Falls)
Beckoning Light (The Afterglow Trilogy #1)
Perilous Light (The Afterglow Trilogy #2)
Enduring Light (The Afterglow Trilogy #3)

www.AlyssaRoseIvy.com
www.facebook.com/AlyssaRoseIvy
twitter.com/AlyssaRoseIvy
AlyssaRoseIvy@gmail.com

Acknowledgements

As always, this book would not have been possible without the support of my family. Grant, you know how much I appreciate everything you do.

Thank you to Jessica Watterson, Katy Austin, Melanie Genanatti, and Whitney Perry for beta reading, and to Jennifer Snyder for being the fantastic writing partner that you are. Thanks to Kris Kendall for your editing, and to Kristina Scheid for the proofreading. Thanks to Claudia of Phatpuppy Art for the beautiful cover design.

Thanks to all the bloggers who have continued to help me spread the word about my books, and to my readers for giving me the opportunity to share another story with you.

Chapter One

Casey

Glowing Eyes. In the chaos of the moment, the only thing I could focus on were the yellow eyes that followed my every move. They were eerie and seemed more at home on an animatronic creation than on the living, breathing animal that had me cornered in the alley. I knew I was stuck, but I didn't think about death. It wasn't an option because I wasn't ready for it. Realistic or not, I was a firm believer that we make our own destiny.

I stepped back, convinced that if I walked backward slowly enough, I'd escape. I silently cursed Eric for making me throw out the trash after my shift. He was such an ass of an assistant manager.

At first, the wolf didn't move—at least I thought it was a wolf, although it seemed two sizes too big. As strange as it should have been to see a giant wolf in an alley, I'd seen far stranger in my nine months of living in New York City.

"Easy boy," I said in a half whisper, more for myself than for the beast now taking slow, deliberate steps toward me.

All of a sudden, he lunged. Gray fur moved in a blur as I blocked my face the best I could in the spilt second I had. A whimper rang out, and I lowered my arms when the contact never came.

The gray wolf slowly limped out of the alley. I searched for an explanation as I struggled to regain my breath and vaguely saw another figure disappear into the distance. He could have been any man, except that in my adrenaline-rich state, I could have sworn he had wings.

My head started to spin, and I reached out for something to hold onto. Then everything went black.

***

"Hey, Bates! Are you okay?"

I forced my eyes open, confused about the cause of my killer headache and the fogginess permeating my head.

"Casey?" Eric bent down next to me with some legitimate concern on his face. "Are you all right?"

"How long have I been out here?" I glanced around, trying to make sense of how I ended up face down in a pile of trash outside my place of work.

"Not too long. When you never came in from tossing the trash I got worried."

Likely. Eric was probably more worried about being named in a potential law suit.

"I'm fine… I think." I struggled to remember what had happened. The only memory I had couldn't be real. It involved a wolf and a strange guy with wings. Evidently I managed to pass out and hit my head on a trash can. Because that's normal.

"Are you sure? Do you think you can walk?"

"Yeah, I can walk." The alternative was to let him carry me inside. Despite his good looks, Eric's personality nullified any desire to have him hold me, even if walking seemed like an insurmountable task at the moment. Out of necessity, I accepted his outstretched hand and leaned heavily on his shoulder. My head continued to throb, and all I wanted to do was get home and lie down.

He put me down on the couch in the break room. The worn sofa wasn't a place I ever wanted to lay my head, considering it was twenty years old and had probably never been cleaned, but I didn't have a choice. The world was spinning.

"Did you hit your head?" Eric asked, taking a seat next to me. His muscular arm blocked my view of the room.

I reached up and touched the knot forming on the back of my head. "Yes. I have no idea how."

"Only you would do something that ridiculous." He routinely made fun of me, but something was off. Then again, I'd hit my head so maybe everything was off.

"Can you get my purse? It's in that locker." I pointed around him to where I'd stowed my stuff.

"Sure." He walked across the room and retrieved my ancient knock-off Gucci. He handed it to me, and I fished out my phone.

"Are you calling someone to get you?" He settled in next to me. The couch sunk down from the extra weight.

"Yeah. My cousin." I hit Rhett's name on my contacts list.

"Casey?" Rhett answered after two rings. Five years older than me, Rhett and I didn't hang out much, but he was being seriously awesome by letting me crash in the spare bedroom (read closet) in his apartment in the Village.

"Any chance you could walk down to Coffee Heaven?"

"Sure…but is there a particular reason why?" He sounded distracted, which probably meant he was buried in his research. A twinge of guilt went through me when I thought about bothering him, but asking Eric to walk me home was out of the question, and we were the only two closing.

"I kind of passed out and hit my head."

"What?" Shuffling, followed by a door slamming, let me know he was on his way. I worked a few blocks from Rhett's place, so I knew it wouldn't be long. "Hold tight. I'll be right there."

"I could have walked you home." Eric stood up, probably getting ready to unlock the front door for Rhett. He opened his mouth like he wanted to say more, but he quickly shut it.

"Rhett doesn't mind."

Eric mumbled something incomprehensible before stomping off through the doorway. I didn't really get him. He was a jerk to me most of the time, but then other times he got almost protective.

Eric returned minutes later with Rhett on his heels.

"You okay, Case?" Rhett kneeled down in front of me. As usual, his brown hair was all rumpled, and it looked like he hadn't showered yet. It was ten o'clock at night.

"I think so."

"What happened to her?" He looked at Eric, an unspoken accusation hanging in the air.

"I'm not positive. She went out to toss the trash and when I came out to look for her, she was on the ground."

"Next time, throw out the trash yourself." Rhett helped me up. "Casey won't be coming in to work tomorrow."

"Hey. I will so. I need the shift." My savings were dwindling, and that didn't bode well for going back to school the next semester.

Rhett shook his head. "No, you don't."

"I do. Eric, don't find someone to cover me. I'll be in."

"See you tomorrow, Bates." Eric blatantly ignored my cousin and called me by my last name. No matter how many times I reminded him that I preferred he use my first name, he disregarded the request.

"Night," I called just before the door closed behind us, leaving us in the brisk night air.

"You're a glutton for punishment, kid."

"Who are you calling kid?" I linked my arm with Rhett's as we walked past Washington Square Park. I was feeling better but was still light headed.

"You're nineteen. You're a kid."

"I don't feel like one." Working full time and trying to support myself on only a step above minimum wage had been an eye opening experience, even with the ridiculously cheap rent I owed Rhett.

"Usually you don't act like one. Rushing to get back to your crap job is acting like a kid."

"It's the only job I have, and I need it." Beggars can't be choosers in New York when it comes to making money with only a high school diploma and almost no previous work experience. Funny how working at a summer camp doesn't do much for a resume.

"Or you could pick a less expensive school and not worry so much about financial aid."

"Says the guy working on his PhD at NYU?"

"Hey, they pay me now." He opened the exterior door to our building.

"They didn't when you were an undergrad."

He let go of me so he could unlock the inner door. You had to tug on the door at the same time you turned the key or it didn't work. The super was supposed to fix the temperamental lock months before. "True, but my scholarship covered most of it."

I stood just inside the entryway. "All right, can't argue with that."

"Can you make it?" He gestured to the stairs. We lived in a third floor walkup.

"Maybe." I headed toward the stairs that currently looked like mountains. "It's worth a try."

Ten minutes later, I was propped up on the couch with a bottle of water. Rhett worried over me for another few minutes before I made him get back to work. I flipped through the channels, hoping for some random movie. There was absolutely nothing on, so I settled for the local news.

Another animal attack has been reported in Bryant Park. Authorities have not released the names of the victims, but once again citizens are urged to use caution when frequenting outdoor areas after dark.

I'd seen two other news reports just like it that week, although both reported attacks in different parts of the city. I thought of the wolf in the alley. It must have just been my overactive imagination messing with me. I needed sleep, and lots of it. I switched off the TV and closed my eyes. I didn't even have the energy to move to my room.

Chapter Two

Casey

There's an art to serving coffee. The trick is knowing what the customer really wants. Putting whipped cream on the wrong person's Macchiato might mean a bad day for both of you. That might seem melodramatic, but I like to keep things as calm as possible.

After six months at Coffee Heaven, I'd gotten used to my regulars. I learned quickly that most wanted the same drink every day, but others changed it up. I had one girl who seriously coordinated her smoothie with her outfit. I had to give her points for creativity.

I did have favorites. Like this old woman, Mrs. Anders, who came in at seven forty-five every morning for a cup of earl gray tea and a bagel. I got to the point where I had her tea waiting for her because I knew she liked to let it cool. My other favorite was a guy. Tall, handsome, and utterly drool worthy, he caught my attention the first time he ordered a coffee. But what stuck with me wasn't his appearance; it was how sad he looked. I'd never seen a guy look that heartbroken day after day.

We never talked much. He'd force a smile when I handed him his coffee and asked how he was, but he never asked me anything back. I should have gotten the hint, but I'm a fairly outgoing person, and he seemed in need of a friend.

The morning after my hallucination in the alley incident, he didn't show up at eight like he usually did. He was twenty minutes late. Having arrived at work at six, I was already regretting my decision to come in. Exhausted and still feeling out of it, I could practically hear Rhett saying "I told you so." We had almost a brother-sister relationship. He was really close with my older sister, and I was the little kid always chasing them around.

"Running behind this morning?" I asked as I placed the piping hot cup of coffee down on the counter. For once, the cup didn't have Toby scrawled on the side. In the rush of the morning, I didn't even have time to add names.

He picked up the coffee without bothering with a cardboard sleeve. He must have had some real heat tolerance. "Yeah, something like that." He hadn't shaved, and the stubble on his face only accentuated his rugged good lucks. A lot of my friends were into pretty boys, but I always preferred my men a little rougher around the edges.

"I'm kind of having a morning like that too. That's why my hair's up." I gestured to where my chestnut brown hair sat piled up into something resembling a bun on the top of my head. I'd barely made it out of bed in time, and anything more than a quick rinse off shower and brushing my teeth was out of the question.

Toby glanced at my hair and then back at my face.

"I usually wear it down..." Evidently he hadn't noticed every little detail about me. To be fair, most people didn't remember every little detail about the person serving their coffee. Still, I'd held out some hope he'd noticed more than my mad skills at filling a paper cup.

He nodded. "Oh. Okay. Cool."

"Yeah. Well, I hope the rest of your day goes better." I smiled, refusing to let his reluctance to talk affect me.

"Thanks. You too." He half waved before walking out the front door. I enjoyed the view of him from behind. He could wear a pair of pants well.

"Man, that guy is hot." My coworker, Remy, picked that moment to turn away from fixing the espresso machine. I'm sure it wasn't random.

"That he is." I tried to hide my disappointment at his disinterest as I helped another few customers, glad that the morning rush was almost over.

"His name's Toby, right?" she asked even though she knew the answer. We'd discussed him on more than a dozen occasions.

"Uh, huh. I guess he kind of looks like a Toby."

She laughed. "Whatever a Toby looks like. I've never met one before."

"You know what? Me either." There was nothing wrong with a less popular name. I kinda liked Casey for that reason. It was common enough that everyone could pronounce it, but I never had to go by Casey B in school or anything.

"Jess and Emmett are having a party tomorrow. Do you want to go?" She referred to our mutual friend from NYU who'd just moved in with her boyfriend. Jess was more her friend than mine, but she seemed pretty nice.

Just another NY suburb kid like me; although she was from Westchester, and I was from Long Island. I'd gotten the sense that she wasn't from tons of money either.

"Sure. Is this a housewarming party or something? Do we need to have a gift?" Always practical, I didn't want to be the rude one who showed up empty handed.

"Hmm, I guess so. I'll get something from my sister's store. I think Jess would like her stuff." Remy's sister owned this cute little boutique that specialized in candles, lampshades, and other household accessories.

"Can I chip in? I don't think I'll have time to stop anywhere." I also didn't have much cash to spare. Remy was usually pretty reasonable with her money so I didn't worry she'd pick out something extravagant.

"Sure. "

Remy was one of my few friends from NYU I still talked to regularly, and that was probably only because we worked together. When my dad lost his job, I made the decision of where to cut back easy on my parents. I took a semester off.

I'd planned on just moving home, but when Rhett offered me the closet, I jumped on it. Moving back home felt like giving up somehow. I'd always wanted to live in the city, and I wasn't willing to let go of that dream just yet. I also wasn't willing to let go of NYU. I'd started working full time with the hopes of making some cash and getting myself categorized as an independent for financial aid. My goal was to return part time in the fall. My back up plan was to apply to a less expensive school, which wouldn't have been the worst option. Still, less expensive school or not, I had to pay my living expenses.

I wanted to see my other friends, but when you leave school, it's sort of hard to stay part of the social scene—not to mention it's kind of depressing. Who would have thought I'd ever be jealous of my friends for having to go to class and study?

"Want to meet at my place and grab dinner before we head over?" Remy rang up a customer. She wore her long, strawberry blonde hair in a braid down her back. I wished I could pull off a braid like that. I just looked like a little kid when I did it. She looked fun.

"Yeah, that sounds good." I wasn't surprised she didn't suggest my apartment. I'd been trying to avoid bringing friends over. Rhett was already doing me a favor. He didn't need a bunch of "kids" messing up his place.

The rest of our shift was uneventful. Remy left at lunch time to get over to campus for class. I tried not to feel too jealous as I wiped down the counters.

"Any big plans this weekend, Bates?" Eric snuck up behind me. He seemed to always wait until I was the only other one working to show his face. I was slightly surprised he hadn't started out by asking about my head, but that was Eric. You never knew what to expect from him.

"Not really."

He leaned back against the counter, his hulking figure boxing me in. "I heard you talking to Remy about a party."

"Were you eavesdropping?"

"No. I was listening to my employees."

"We're not your employees."

"You work *under* me." He accentuated the word under, and it kind of made my skin crawl. At twenty-three, Eric wasn't that much older than my nineteen, but that didn't mean his pseudo come-ons didn't skeeve me out. There was something almost menacing about him. You knew he was dangerous just by being near him. Why someone like that would be an assistant manager at a coffee shop, I didn't know. But he did moonlight as a bouncer.

"Is there a point to this questioning?" Letting someone know they intimidate you is never a good idea. I tried to make myself appear unmoved.

"Come out with me Saturday night." He crossed his arms over his unbelievably built chest. No one could say Eric wasn't in shape. However, they might question his use of performance enhancement drugs.

"Didn't you just say I was your employee?"

"Yes."

"So…doesn't that seem like a conflict of interest?"

He ran a hand through his blond hair. "It would only be a conflict of interest if you said no."

"How do you figure?" I crossed my arms.

"I can make your life easy or hard, Bates."

"This is harassment."

"And what are you going to do about it?" A light smile tugged on the corner of his lips.

"Report it. Marv won't put up with it." The owner was a hell of a lot nicer than Eric was.

His smile became a full on grin. "My uncle doesn't have a problem with me dating you."

"Excuse me? Uncle?"

"Yeah. He's my mom's brother. That's why we don't have the same last name."

"Oh." Damn it. How had I not figured that out before? The more I thought about, the more it fit. They definitely had a close relationship.

"So Saturday, eight o'clock?"

"No."

"Excuse me?"

"I said no. I'm not going out with you." I couldn't afford to lose the job, but losing my dignity would be worse. I wasn't going to let someone bully me.

"Is there a reason you're being a bitch?" He stood up straight, accentuating his height.

"Is there a reason you can't take no for an answer?"

He laughed. "I like your spirit, Bates."

"My spirit?"

"Yeah. I might even respect it a little." He shifted and gave me a smidge more personal space.

"Okay…so that means you'll back off?"

"It means I'm going to pretend you didn't just say no. I'll pick you up at eight Saturday."

I stood up as straight as possible, trying to make my 5'7" seem even taller. "Do you think I want to keep this job that bad?"

"I think you want to put your own roof over your head so you don't have to run home to mommy and daddy." He relaxed his arms down at his sides.

His statement about picking me up set in. "How do you know where I live?"

"Your employee file."

"That's private."

"Is it Casey Morgan Bates?" He winked. "I'm out, see you Saturday night."

"I'm not going out with you!" I yelled, but he didn't glance back as he slipped outside.

Perfect.

Chapter Three

Toby

"You've got to come tonight." Emmett's voice echoed across the gym. We were shooting hoops like two old friends. No one would imagine the history between us—not even him.

"Why?" I caught a rebound and easily tossed it through the net.

"Because you've been moping around about Allie long enough. She moved on. So should you." Just the mention of Allie's name made my chest tighten. Getting over an ex-girlfriend is hard, but try getting over her when you work for her fiancé.

"I don't get it, man. You could have any girl you want. You live in a fucking penthouse for God's sake, yet you never date."

"You wouldn't get it." I went for a jump shot, using only a quarter as much effort as I'd use if it were just me in the gym.

"I wouldn't? If you were still into her, why did you dump her to begin with?" Emmett's sneakers squeaked on the polished wood floor.

The side effect of having a witch erase your friend's memory is that she might erase more than you want her to. It isn't something I'd have ever agreed to if I thought there was another choice, but the other option was a one way trip to the morgue for both Emmett and his girlfriend.

"She dumped me, man." I caught the rebound and took another shot.

"Oh? Really?" His blank stare backed up my discovery that every memory he had involving Allie was now a little mixed up. I felt guilty about messing with his memories and holding him and Jess hostage, but in the end, things worked out for the two of them. Besides, it was either kidnap them or let my grandfather destroy the girl I loved. I couldn't sit back and allow that no matter how much I hated treating my friends that way.

"Yes, really. She dumped me, and now she's engaged. I'm allowed to be pissed." I tossed the ball to Emmett.

"Pissed. Sure. But not pathetic. Come over. Who knows, maybe you'll meet someone."

"Yeah, yeah. Just because you're getting ready to propose doesn't mean the rest of the world wants that bull shit." Falling in love once was bad enough. I had no intention of doing it again.

"Will you come or not?" He went for a shot but missed the basket.

"I'll come." I caught the rebound and easily tossed it through the net again.

"Cool. You need the address?"

I smiled to myself. I knew the address since I was the one who found the apartment for them. Neither of them seemed to think it was odd that they were paying a fraction of the price they should have to live in that kind of place. Messing with people's memories seems to be fraught with side effects. "I've got the address." I may have kidnapped them for a little while, but I was paying them back in the only way I could—with money.

"Awesome. Jess is inviting a bunch of her friends from school. Maybe one will catch your eye."

"Doubtful." If I was looking for a girlfriend, it wouldn't be a college girl. One of the benefits of dropping out of Princeton was avoiding that crowd. Agreeing to the party aside, it wasn't my scene anymore. I'd never pictured myself the drop out type, but I couldn't live in Princeton and work my job in New York. Something had to give.

I sensed my cousins before I saw them. I'd always had stronger senses than other people. Even before I really understood what I was, I knew where the trait came from. My mom's family.

"What do you two want?" I took another shot without turning around. I could have whispered and they would have still heard me.

"We've got a problem." Tim sat down on the bottom bleacher. He was the older of the two and the more talkative. Tom never said much. I'd kind of inherited the henchman when I took over for my grandfather, but they came in handy—sometimes.

I let Emmett grab the rebound, and I joined them by the bleachers. "What's the problem?" I knew it had something to do with the attacks, but I didn't know what.

"The count is up."

"Fantastic. Same signs?" I spoke as vaguely as possible. Emmett's mind may have been toyed with, but that didn't mean he was completely dumb.

"Yeah. We can't keep ignoring this."

He was right, whether I wanted to admit it or not. "Give me ten. I need to shower."

"No prob, boss." Tom and Tim stood up at the same time and headed to the exit. "Meet you at the office."

"Is everything okay, man?" Emmett set aside an empty bottle of water he'd gulped down in less than a minute.

"Yeah. It's just work stuff."

"They work you to the bone."

"They pay well." The excuse sounded believable to my own ears.

He dribbled the ball. "That's something. So we'll see you tonight?"

"I'll be there." I nodded before heading into the locker room. Surprise, surprise, it was time to go back to work.

***

At least my office had a good view. That's what I told myself when I dragged my ass into work every day. That way I could pretend I was just like every other sucker out there, going to work just so I could pay the bills. But that wasn't me. I didn't have a normal job, and I had enough money to pay my bills for the rest of my life. I'd inherited my grandfather's position and taken on a new one for the king, otherwise known as the guy who stole my girlfriend. Needless to say, I wasn't thrilled with the situation, but it wasn't the kind of offer you turned down. Besides, my nature wouldn't let me. The drive for power was in my blood.

"So what's the update?" I took a seat at my giant mahogany desk. It was way too big and old fashioned for my taste, but updating my office wasn't a priority. I still hadn't even gone back to Princeton to pack up my dorm room. There wasn't anything I wanted from it. The only personal mementos I had there were pictures of Allie and my mom. I didn't particularly want either.

"They're moving outside the city." Tim paced the room. "We're not going to be able to hide them anymore."

"And we're sure it's shifters? There's no other explanation?" I knew the answer, but my life would have been much easier if it had been a different one.

"Yes. You know it as much as I do." He leaned one hand on a bookcase. His brown hair appeared almost red in the late day sun that was spilling in through the window.

"How big is this? Is it just one wolf pack or several?"

Tim paused for a beat. "It's also bears."

"Bears?" I asked with genuine surprise.

"Yeah. It's got to be them. That's the only explanation for what happened at Forest Hills."

"You almost make it sound like wolves and bears are working together." I flipped through a pile of papers on my desk. You'd think in the digital age, we'd be done with paperwork.

"Crazy, I know. But it can't be a coincidence."

"What are they trying to accomplish? Lower shifters can be reckless, but they usually avoid violence for violence sake, and they don't want to get The Society's attention."

"Unless that is what they want."

"They want to get attention." The reality dawned on me. "They want to get everyone's attention."

"Why? Just to stir up trouble?"

"Who knows." I thought about the wolf I'd caught the other night outside the coffee shop. When he chose Casey, he'd made it personal. That barista was the one bright spot of my day. I weighed the pros and cons of telling my cousins about it. The pros won out. "I caught a wolf the other night."

"You what?" Tom surprised me by speaking.

"He was about to attack a human outside a coffee house in the Village."

"What did you do with him? You killed him, I hope." Tim took a seat in one of the visitor chairs. They were covered in brown leather and starting to show their age. That oversight wasn't like my grandfather.

"I doubt he's shifting back." It's hard for shifters to heal in their animal form. I didn't do him any favors.

Tim shuddered. "I'd hate to get on your bad side, cuz."

"Then don't." I was kind of enjoying the reputation I'd developed after killing my grandfather with my bare hands. Everyone thought I was ruthless and seemed to be scared of me. What they didn't realize is I'd only acted on instinct. I had to protect Allie in any way I could.

Tim faked a laugh. Always the kiss up. "Of course. So what do you suggest? Is it time to bring in the king?"

I sighed. "I'd like to avoid that as long as possible." In addition to inheriting my grandfather's position, I was also the leader of the New York contingent of The Society. Most humans have never heard of The Society, mostly because they aren't important enough. Any paranormal or other supernatural being, or high ranking member of the human race, is well aware that The Society is the group that calls all the shots.

"Is this because of your personal issues with the king?"

"Personal issues?" I guess you could call the fact that the king had taken my girlfriend as his mate a personal issue.

"Levi's king now, and he even gave you a good gig. Cut the guy some slack."

"He gave me this *gig* because I protected Allie."

Tim looked away, and I knew he was rolling his eyes. "However you spin it, he gave you some power. Embrace it. The city is ours."

"Yeah. Just a few months in and all hell has broken loose. It's like everyone was waiting for the old man to die before digging in."

The brothers looked at each other.

"You think that's what it is?"

"Of course. The lower shifters think we're weak. We have to remind them we're Pterons, and we don't take their shit."

"And how do you suggest we do that?"

"Either you let us have our fun, or we call in the king."

I didn't need to think over the options for long. "Have your fun, but keep it clean. No humans get hurt."

"Got it. You want to join us?"

"No. I've got plans tonight." Maybe there was something positive about agreeing to Emmett's party. I had no desire to watch my cousins knock around a bunch of idiot shifters who thought that flexing their muscles was going to make a difference. If there's anything that Pteron's hate, it's lower shifters causing trouble. We may have been shifters ourselves, but we were a hell of a lot stronger, faster, and smarter. That didn't mean that anyone wanted to listen to us—but they always did.

Pterons have been running The Society worldwide for centuries. The North American region has been run by the Laurent family out of New Orleans for several generations. Levi, the current king and the bane of my existence, had just taken his place a few months before. The last time I'd seen Allie was at their coronation. She looked so happy that I decided to stay the hell away. Seeing each other wasn't good for either of us, especially not me. With millions of human girls out there, Pterons date and mate with humans almost exclusively, I could have found someone new, but I wasn't ready yet. At least that's what I told myself.

By the time my cousins left, the sun had set, and the city was dark once again. I loved the night for one reason, and I was about to enjoy it.

I headed up to the roof, unbuttoning my shirt in the process. By the time I pushed through the door into the night, I had already shed the blue fabric. After checking that no one was around, I let myself transform. My large brown wings were easily concealed inside small slits when I wanted them to be, but it was always invigorating to have them out. Nothing felt quite as good as flying, and I did it every chance I had.

I jumped off the side of the building, falling for a moment before climbing again to make sure no one noticed. I headed away from the lights of the city, away from the stress and the constant reminders that I was completely alone.

Chapter Four

Jared

"When did this city get so boring?" I leaned back against the black leather couch in my apartment. I'd been living there since sophomore year of college, and graduation was only a few months away. I needed to find a new place to live, preferably somewhere without roommates. At twenty-two, I was ready for my own space.

"When you finally slept with every girl in the whole damn place." Owen, my roommate, tossed his controller on the ground. He was in an uncharacteristically pissed off mood.

"I haven't slept with them all, but I'll agree I've gone through most of the good ones."

"And you wonder why half the girls at Tulane want you dead."

"Have I ever wondered that?" I smirked. My smirk always pissed Owen off. If he was already in a bad mood, I might as well make it worse. That probably makes me seem like an ass, but it's just the way it was with us. We'd been butting heads since preschool. He knew as well as I did that a few angry girls didn't bother me. I'd been spending a lot of time with the Loyola girls lately. There's just something about catholic school girls…

"Two more months and we're done with school. I'm sure you'll find plenty of excuses to leave New Orleans."

"Depends. Levi's been keeping me busy." I stretched my arms above my head. I needed to get a good work out in. That was probably Owen's problem. Pterons tend to get cranky when we don't get enough physical exercise. Maybe it's because we descend from bird shifters—the whole stretch your wings thing.

"Yeah, because he was dumb enough to make you head of security."

"You're his chief advisor. What does that say about the new king?"

Owen grinned. "That he's very well advised."

"Let's hope he doesn't actually need your sorry ass."

"I wouldn't worry."

"I'm not worrying. Levi doesn't care about much that doesn't involve Allie." Levi had been my other roommate until recently. He'd gone from prince to king and was living in a mansion with his mate. Although I found Allie to be annoying when I first met her, she'd grown on me. We'd fallen into a weird sort of friendship that worked for us.

"Can you really blame him after all the hell he went through to get her?" Owen grabbed a soda from the fridge.

Allie put Levi through the ringer when he was trying to get her to become his queen. Her resistance had made him miserable, but in the end, I got the sense that it made them stronger.

"No...but eventually he's got to get tired of fucking the same girl constantly, right?"

"That is the queen you're talking about."

"Really? I didn't know that." I got off the couch and headed into the kitchen.

"I'm just saying, Levi can't get tired of her."

"I'm just saying, eventually he's going to have to come up for air." I opened a beer.

Owen laughed. "I'm sure Levi would love to know you want his sex life to suck."

"I don't even want to talk about it anymore. We need to go do something though. Where do you want to go?"

"Isn't the question who do you want to do? Are you looking for a tourist or a coed?"

"Does it matter?"

"Is this your version of depression? You no longer care what girl you screw?"

"Shut up, dip shit."

"Not a chance."

"Let's go to The Boot." I suggested Tulane's "campus bar" not because I particularly enjoyed the atmosphere, but because it was the fall back option on Tuesdays. Fifty cent night made it a happening place.

"Why not." Owen scooped his keys off the counter, knowing we wouldn't be coming back together. When possible, I went home with the girl. It made it easier to slip out in the morning.

The Boot was as packed as usual, but it wasn't hard to find a table. Humans tended to stay out of our way, thanks to a combination of good sense and our reputation.

"I'll grab us a pitcher of something." Owen headed for the bar while I took a seat at the table. I wasn't looking forward to drinking the cheap beer, but it was all part of the experience.

"Hi." A cute enough redhead walked over. I could see her group of friends watching her approach.

"Hi." You never wanted to seem over eager.

"My friends and I were wondering if we could sit with you?" She twirled a strand of her hair around her finger nervously.

I glanced over at her friends. There was a blonde I wouldn't mind talking to. "Sure."

The girl ran back over to her friends, and they took seats just as Owen returned with two pitchers. "Glad I grabbed two."

I gave him a look the girls probably didn't notice. At least they'd kill the time.

"I'm Ava, and these are Jackie and Katie." The redhead introduced her blonde and brunette friends. They each smiled shyly. Clearly, Ava was the outgoing one of the group, which explained why she approached me first.

"I'm Jared and this is Owen." I nodded to Owen who was already getting lost in his glass.

"Cool. What year are you guys?" Ava moved her attention between the two of us.

"Seniors," Owen answered without looking up.

"That's awesome. Do you have cars?" The blonde, I couldn't remember if that one was Jackie or Katie, asked.

Owen groaned quietly enough that only I could hear. These girls were freshman. At one time, I would have been glad for that. They were the easiest mark, but now I was tired of them. Maybe I was getting old.

I smiled at Owen and decided I might as well have some fun with them. "Yes, and we even have drivers licenses."

Jackie or Katie laughed. "Yeah, we figured that."

"That was a joke." I poured myself a cup, not bothering to offer any to the girls. We wouldn't be staying long.

Owen pulled out his cell. "Just got a text from Anne. She wanted to see if I could give her a ride to Target."

I laughed. "And you're going to do it, aren't you?" Owen had a soft spot for this little friend of Allie's.

"Am I doing anything more interesting here?" He spoke quietly, still concerned with hurting the feelings of the girls across from us. They were whispering, but I could hear them clearly. They were deciding whether they should ask if we had a third friend. What were they, twelve? If we'd been interested, sharing wouldn't have been a problem.

"I'll join you." I pushed away my nearly untouched cup. "Excuse me, ladies."

"Are you guys leaving?" Ava asked.

"Yeah, we've got to be somewhere. Enjoy the beer though."

"Oh. Bye." She didn't bother to hide her disappointment. Either did I. Was I really choosing a Target run over flirting with girls?

Chapter Five

Casey

Rhett took a break from packing to ask me the same question for the millionth time. "Are you sure you're feeling better? You still look a little out of it."

"I'm fine. Just tired. You need to go on this trip."

"I could probably postpone." He tossed more clothes into his worn out black duffel. Even my luggage was in better shape.

"And what did you do before you started babysitting me?" I took a seat on the one clear spot on his double bed. For such a nerdy guy, Rhett liked his clothes. I packed lighter than he did.

He grunted something unintelligible involving frustration and my name.

"I'm an adult, and I promise not to throw any huge parties or anything."

He scowled. "Glad to know you're going to miss me."

"You know I will. Look at it this way, I'm a built in house sitter."

"Don't do anything stupid, Case." He pushed his wire rim glasses back up on his face. He usually wore contacts, but he didn't bother with them when he got busy with research. I couldn't relate. I had 20/20 vision.

"I won't, but I've got to go. I'm late to meet Remy for dinner." I stood up.

He hugged me. "Call me if anything comes up. I'll still get service in Russia."

"Good to know. If you decide to run off with a Russian girl, at least send me a letter so I can live vicariously through your adventures."

He laughed. "You're so weird."

"Maybe I learned it from you."

"Or from Vera. You get more and more like her every day."

"Yeah. Maybe." I turned and left. I wasn't in the mood to discuss my older sister.

***

"I still can't believe Eric did that to you." Remy brought Eric up for the third time that night. I'd told her more as a warning than anything, but she wasn't letting it go. She'd told the whole restaurant about it at dinner. Remy had the kind of voice that carried. It didn't help that the whole way over to Jess' I felt like someone was watching me. I was losing my mind.

"He's an ass. Why does it surprise you?" I took a long sip from my red cup and set it aside on the end table. Like everything else in the apartment, the furniture was steps above the usual college grade stuff the rest of us lived on.

Maybe their parents' paid for the place. The rent had to be steep. Two bedrooms, with an eat-in kitchen and a giant living room, the square footage was almost unheard of in my group of friends. Add in that it was a doorman building, and you were talking serious cash.

"Still…why now? Why wait six months?" Remy always liked to find an ulterior meaning in things. If a professor called on someone first, it was because he played favorites. If a customer ordered a different drink, they were going through some existential crisis, and so on.

"I don't know. Maybe he's just bored or hard up for girls or something." I did find it surprising that he'd gone as far as picking an actual time. His teasing had been more general before. Maybe now that we'd been working together so much, he felt he could be more forward. No matter the reason, I didn't like it.

"Who's hard up for girls?" Jess asked, flipping her blonde hair off her shoulder before settling on the arm of a red love seat. She was one of those ultra-pretty girls who knew it. She could get any guy she wanted, but she'd settled on her high school sweetheart. Emmett seemed like a nice enough guy, and he was definitely crazy about her. I had a feeling there was a sparkly ring in her near future.

I crossed my legs, already antsy to get up off the couch and move again. "Just this jerk at work."

"Is he cute?" Jess laughed. "Just kidding. If he's bugging you, why not tell your boss?"

"He kind of is my boss, and the only one he answers to is his uncle."

"Oh…that's not good." She gave me a sympathetic look.

"What? Marv is Eric's uncle?" Remy had a similar reaction to me. At least I wasn't the only one who'd failed to pick up on that detail.

I nodded. "Weird, isn't it?" Then I turned back to Jess. "It's not good at all. I'm hoping it was only talk and he doesn't actually show up tomorrow night."

"Just have Rhett send him away," Remy suggested.

"He's leaving in the morning for Russia."

"Oh yeah. I forgot about that." She twisted off the cap of her beer.

"Just make sure you're out then, Casey. Make plans so when he shows up, you aren't home." Jess nibbled on some tortilla chips.

I liked the suggestion in theory. "Do you have any big plans I can jump in on, Remy?"

She blushed. "I actually have a date."

"With who? Is it that guy from your chem class?" Jess asked. I'd had no idea Remy liked a guy from chem. I was really out of the loop.

"Yeah...believe it or not, I asked him out."

"Nice. Way to make the first move." I patted her on the back. She was usually nervous about approaching guys, so it was a pretty huge step for her. "I'll find something to do."

"We could make plans," a somewhat familiar male voice asked.

I craned my neck behind me, curious who the voice belonged to.

"Toby? Hi." I tried to take my jaw off the floor as I scrambled from the couch. My favorite customer was standing in front of me. Had he just asked me out?

"You're Casey, right?" He studied me, his brown eyes giving me no hint of what was going on in his head.

"Yeah." I was honestly surprised he knew my name.

"You two know each other?" Jess asked, looking from Toby and then back to me with a very amused smile on her face.

"She serves good coffee." Toby smiled. It was one of those forced half smiles of his, but it was something.

"He means I can pour coffee into a cup."

Jess laughed, and the slightly high-pitched tone of it made me think of tiny pixies or fairies. "What a small world."

"I guess so." He shrugged. "So what do you say? Want to make plans?"

"Why?"

His face scrunched up in thought a little. "Do you usually make guys explain their interest this early on?"

Jess laughed again. This time louder. "I guess Casey's playing hard to get."

I sipped the orange substance resembling a screw driver that was currently in my plastic cup. "What would you want to do?"

"I don't know. Maybe we can do dinner."

"Oh. Sure." Was I really planning a date with Toby? "Where should I meet you?"

"I can just pick you up."

"Oh, you don't have to do that."

"Really, I don't mind at all," he insisted.

I needed to find out how well Jess knew this guy before I shared my address. I glanced at her, and she pretty much read my mind. "Did you know that Toby and I went to high school together? He dated my best friend."

Toby paled. "Here's my number. Call me when you decide." He slipped a thick, cream-colored business card into my right hand. In the process, his fingers touched mine and we looked at each other. I wondered if he enjoyed the momentary contact as much as I did.

"Sure. I'll call you."

He nodded before leaving. I waited for him to turn around to look at me again, but he didn't. He just walked right through the doorway.

"Toby just asked you out." Remy grinned.

"Technically, he asked if I wanted to make plans."

"He asked you out," Jess said excitedly. She was one of those bubbly types whose excitement was kind of contagious.

I let myself enjoy it. "All right, he did."

Jess bounced a little in her seat. "I wonder where he's going to take you? You know he's loaded, right?"

"Really?" He wore suits all the time, but that didn't mean he was rich. I'd always assumed he was older.

"Yeah. He has some family business that he runs. He was one of the wealthier guys in high school, but not like he is now. It's like his funds are unlimited."

"Unlimited?" I wasn't sure how I felt about the new info. I didn't want to change the way I felt about a guy just because he was rich, but it made any real relationship seem less likely. Maybe I was getting ahead of myself anyway. It was only dinner.

"Hot, rich, and single?" Remy grinned. "And I thought those guys were extinct."

I shrugged. "Evidently they buy their coffee at Coffee Heaven."

Emmett joined us, handing Jess another drink. "Did Toby leave already?"

Jess leaned into Emmett's arm. "Yeah…but not before asking Casey out."

"Seriously?" Emmett grinned at me. "Nice. Be easy on him. He's a bit out of practice."

I wasn't sure if he was referring to dating or sex. I had no desire to ask for clarification. "So you all went to high school together?"

"Yeah. Toby and I go way back."

"Is he in school, or does he just work?" I wondered if he went to Fordham with Emmett. I'd never seen him around NYU, but that didn't mean he didn't go there.

"No. He started out at Princeton first semester, but then he dropped out."

"Was it because of a girl?" His reaction to the mention of an ex-girlfriend made his somber mood understandable.

Jess nodded. "It's weird because he dumped her. She had a hard time getting over it, but she's moved on. She's actually engaged already."

"Want to know something funny?" Emmett shifted so Jess was practically sitting on his lap. "Toby tried to tell me that Allie was the one who dumped him. Isn't that crazy?"

Jess looked at him with a funny expression."Definitely crazy. That's kind of a big detail to mix up. The whole reason we went down to New Orleans was to help her forget him."

"Does she still live around here?" I asked.

"No. Allie goes to Tulane. We went down to New Orleans for the summer and she never left."

Phew. At least I didn't need to worry about running into this ex-girlfriend.

"Do you know why they broke up?" If he dumped her, why was he so upset when people brought up her name?

"I don't remember. They were really serious, but then out of the blue, it was over." Jess looked lost in thought. "It's weird, I can't remember any of the details anymore. Sometimes I feel like my brain's all messed up."

"That makes two of us. Maybe we should lay off all the alcohol." Emmett looked down at his nearly empty beer.

"Oh…" I was positive there was a story behind the breakup, but it wasn't the time or place to push for more answers. Besides, it didn't look like Jess or Emmett had any.

"I can't believe you're going out with him. You've been eying Toby for months." Remy grinned. Of course she brought the conversation back to our date again.

"Oh. I thought you just served him coffee." Jess raised an eyebrow.

I shrugged. "I plead the fifth."

Chapter Six

Toby

Had I really just asked out Casey? I didn't think it through at all. I just didn't like hearing that worry in her voice, especially when I realized who was behind it. I'd started visiting Coffee Heaven after meeting the owner, Marv, at a Society meeting. Coffee Heaven was run by a family of bears (or as they liked to call themselves, Ursus) that were usually pretty loyal. Still, if bears were in on any of the attacks, which I knew they were, Marv's family would know about it. I didn't like the idea of the one bright spot of my day walking into a mess.

By lunch time, the fact that she hadn't called was starting to bother me. I debated asking Emmett for her number, but I didn't want to come on too strong. I just had to wait it out. I squeezed the blue stress ball my grandfather had left behind. It burst open, making an annoying popping sound.

"Staring at that phone isn't going to make it ring." Tim interrupted my thoughts. He'd walked into my office unannounced—again.

"Do you have an update for me?" I tossed the remnants of the ball over my shoulder into the trash.

"It's bigger than we thought."

I sat up straighter. This wasn't good. "In what way?"

"At least four wolf packs and several bear clans are involved. I've also heard there may be some panthers, but I can't be sure." Tim slumped down in his usual chair in front of my desk.

"Fuck."

"My thoughts exactly. We're talking the entire tri-state area and then some."

"Do you know what they want? Do they think we're going to just turn over the city to them?" I felt my anger boiling. I used to be so good at controlling it, but not anymore.

"It's more than the city. They're thinking big picture."

"Who's behind it?" I leaned back in my chair. This job was becoming such a headache.

"Not who you think."

"What do you mean?"

"It's the Galvinos." Tim looked at me nervously.

"Marv's clan?"

"Yes."

I slammed my fist on the desk. "They've always been trustworthy."

"I know. Why do you think I said it's not who you think?" Tim paced. He didn't like delivering bad news. "They have to be working for someone bigger, but right now, all the trails are leading to them."

"I need a meeting with Marv." For more than one reason. Were they the ones who set the wolf on Casey? I already wanted to tear Eric a new one for letting her go out in a dark alley alone at night, but to think he may have known what awaited her. I couldn't hold off the transformation. I felt my back prickle, and I knew my eyes were probably changing color already.

"Whoa, cuz. Calm down." Tim stood up, readying himself for a fight.

I shook myself, breathing slowly, trying to come back around. "A meeting. Set up a meeting."

"Here or on their turf?"

"Neutral. Set something up for tomorrow. I have plans tonight."

"Two nights in a row?" Tim smirked. "Is that an all-time record?"

"Just shut up and get me that meeting."

I got up and looked out the window at the people outside. None of them were worried about crazy bears and wolves trying to take over the city. How had my life gotten so damn complicated so fast? Nineteen wasn't supposed to suck so much.

My phone rang and I grabbed for it, hoping the unknown 631 number was the call I was waiting for.

"Toby here." I used my business greeting without thinking.

"Ah hey. It's Casey." She sounded different on the phone, more timid maybe.

"Hey. I was wondering if you were ever going to call." I tried for nonchalant.

"Yeah, I worked most of the day."

"You work on Saturdays?" Had I known that, I would have gone in to see her. It would have simplified things.

"Usually. I also work a lot of Sundays."

Maybe I'd have to start going over to Coffee Heaven seven days a week. "Good to know."

"Why? You planning to come in on weekends now?"

I smiled. She'd gotten that right. "Like I said last night, you serve good coffee."

"Do you still want to hang out?" She sounded kind of nervous, like she thought I was going to back out.

"Yeah. Definitely. Have you decided whether I can pick you up?"

"Jess says I can trust you. But can we do coffee instead of dinner?"

"And you trust Jess?" I wasn't sure how close they really were. I'd never heard Jess talk about Casey before. I knew the coffee instead of dinner trick was to make it easier for her to leave if things got awkward. I was okay with that. I'd just make sure things ran smoothly.

"I think I do."

I laughed. "Either way, you can trust me." And even if you don't, I already know where you live. I kept that part to myself. I also didn't voice the part about following her home the night before to make sure she was okay. She'd probably interpret my protectiveness as stalking.

"You can't be worse than Eric."

I frowned. What kind of trouble had he been giving her?

She gave me her address and I pretended to jot it down. "Coffee sounds great. I'll see you at seven."

"Great. See you then."

***

Casey was waiting for me outside when I got there.

"Am I late?" I glanced at my watch. I'd made sure to leave extra time.

"No." She looked away guiltily. "I just thought I'd meet you out here."

"And here I thought you trusted me."

She shrugged. "My dad raised me to be careful around men."

"That's a good thing."

We turned the corner and started walking down MacDougal Street in the opposite direction of Coffee Heaven. Even if it weren't run by bears, I wasn't taking her to the place she worked for a date.

"Where are we going?"

"Just a little café I know about." What I left out was that it was a paranormal place with a strict 'no humans without an escort' policy. Hopefully, she wouldn't notice anything different about the clientele. The upside for me was that we'd get a private table with a view. If she wanted a coffee date, she'd get it, but it wasn't going to be anything run of the mill.

Three blocks further down, I hailed a cab. I didn't want to do it too close to her place. There were so many eyes on me at any time, and there was no reason to make it that easy.

"We're taking a cab? There're plenty of good places right here."

"I think you'll like this one." I held open the door to the yellow cab idling at the curb.

"If you say so." She slipped in, and I followed her.

I gave the driver the address of the café, which also happened to be the address of Battery Park. It wasn't too long of a cab ride.

We walked around for a while, and I was thankful that the night was a little bit warmer than the previous few. Spring hadn't come early, and I didn't want Casey getting cold.

"How did I not know there was a second café here?" She gazed around at the gardens like a kid in a candy store. I made a mental note that she liked flowers.

"I guess you haven't been with the right company." Of course, it didn't hurt that the café, The Sprite House, was hidden by spells. Some Pterons stay away from magic, but I embrace it. Maybe it's because I didn't grow up in the supernatural world. I was only introduced in my early teens.

After giving her some time to enjoy the courtyard, I gently led her through the door. We walked up a spiral staircase to the main floor. The entry to the café was decorated in different shades of gold and red. The color theme extended to the elaborate chandeliers that hung down from the ceiling.

Casey eyed me skeptically. "I thought you agreed to a coffee date."

"This is a coffee date. I promise."

I put my hand on the small of her back and directed us to the hostess stand. "Table for two."

"Right this way, sir." The blonde haired witch smiled as she led us through the main section of the room. The café served coffee and dessert until ten o'clock at which point it switched over to a night club. Designed for privacy, it was one large circle with a dozen smaller circles surrounding it. The hostess left us in our own little alcove. Instead of chairs, it was set up as a booth with only one bench. The hostess had correctly assumed this was a date and not business.

I gestured for Casey to scoot in first, both to give her the window, and because I liked the idea of blocking her from the line of sight of anyone passing by. I didn't expect trouble in the café, but you never knew what was going to happen.

I opened one of the black leather menus and set it in front of her. "They have some pretty good specialty coffees here, and the crème brulee is the best I've had."

She leaned in toward me, her shoulder bumping into mine. I savored the closeness. It had been ages since I'd been that close to a girl, let alone one as beautiful as Casey. A few minutes into our date, and I was already berating myself for not asking her out sooner. Even her scent made me happy. The smell wasn't perfume. I figured it was probably body wash. Strawberry.

"Have you had the vanilla storm coffee before?" She used her pointer finger to mark the spot on the menu. The remnants of some sort of light pink polish remained on a few of her nails.

"No, but it sounds good."

"Want to order that for two?" She glanced up at me. "It's funny that you have to order things that way."

"Sure, sounds good. " I didn't mention that they had different types of menus. The witch had slipped us one that only offered larger portion beverages—designed for intimate dates.

As soon as the waitress arrived, I ordered the vanilla storm and a crème brulee to share. By Casey's smile, she agreed with the dessert order.

She settled back against the pillows lining our bench seat and gazed outside. The sun was just going down, creating an orange-red glow across the sky that nearly lit up the window. I assumed the witches were accentuating it somehow, but Casey was transfixed so I was glad for it.

Our waitress brought over our order and Casey tore her eyes away from the sunset. "You definitely know how to pick a place."

"Thanks." I smiled. "I try."

"They take this whole 'for two' thing seriously." She warily picked up the two handled container of coffee.

I laughed. "We don't have to drink it at the same time or anything."

"Yeah, that wasn't going to happen." Her expression was light as she lifted the cup and brought it to her lips. She let out a soft moan that made me wonder what a much louder moan caused by something else entirely would sound like. "This is heavenly."

I took the outstretched cup from her. I sipped the coffee, and she was right. "Very good."

"I wonder why they call it a storm?"

"I don't know, but I doubt they'll tell us. They're pretty secretive about recipes here."

"Oh." Some disappointment crossed her face, and I knew I'd get the recipe sooner or later. "Well, then, we might have to come back." She accepted the cup from me and took another sip. After she gave off another of those small moans, I got a little suspicious.

"Would you excuse me for a minute?"

She nodded, going in for yet another sip.

I found the witch that owned the place, the same one who'd seated us. "What did you put in our coffee?"

She smiled. "You shouldn't have tasted anything different, sir."

"But she's tasting something different, isn't she?" I nodded over my shoulder.

"I thought I'd help you out a little. Push things in the right direction." She rolled her tongue over her teeth.

"It's an aphrodisiac spell?"

"The spell only affects women. I know The Society rules about using magic on Pterons."

"Now what do I do? I can't take it away from her, but I can't let her drink it."

"Why not? You can take her home after this."

I shook my head. "This better not happen again or I'll close this place down."

"You could thank me." She wore a playful look, and I was certain this wasn't the first time she'd used the spell on a customer.

"Thank you?" Witches were usually okay, but this one was earning a spot on my bad side.

"For helping out. It's been too long. Allie's gone, it's time to find someone new." She spoke as though we were close friends and she knew exactly what I was going through. The reality was, we'd only met a handful of times.

I knew the action was done with the right intentions, but it really put me in a bad place. Now even if the opportunity arose, I couldn't ask Casey to go back to my place. I sure as hell wasn't going to take advantage of her that way.

"Relax, Toby. It only works if the girl's into you already. If she isn't, it will be useless. If it works well, you know you've got her attention even without the spell."

"I could kill you for this," I muttered before returning to the table to find Casey with a nearly empty cup and half the pot of crème brulee.

"Sorry I started on this without you." She pushed the dish toward me.

"It's okay." I put an arm behind her and she happily snuggled into my side. I figured letting her get close wasn't taking advantage of her.

"I'm glad you asked me out." She ran a finger down my chest, and even through the cotton of my shirt, it made me shiver with a mix of anticipation and need. "I've wanted this for a long time."

"Me too, but it's getting late."

"Are you ready to go home?" Her words were innocent enough, but her eyes weren't. She wasn't planning on spending the night in her own bed, which made it that much more important that she did.

"Unfortunately, I have to run into work. I'll make sure you get home safe first though."

"Really? That's not fun." She pouted. Then she looped one leg over my lap and straddled me. Her fingers moved to my shirt again, but this time they didn't stop at my chest. I stilled her hand before she could start playing with my belt buckle.

"How about we go out another night? Maybe next week?" I wasn't against using her state to my advantage by lining up a future date. Hopefully she'd remember we made one.

"I'd love to. But do we have to wait that long?" Her teeth nipped my ear. "Can't you just put off work a little bit longer?"

"It's going to be a busy week for me." And a painful night. I'd never hated my jeans more. "But I'll see you at work."

"At work?" she purred into my ear. "Can't it be at play?"

What kind of spell had they used? Casey was ready to go right there at the café. I had to cool things down and fast.

"Not yet." I carefully moved her off my lap and stood up.

The physical separation seemed to help a little. Her face relaxed, and she rested her hands at her sides. "Okay. Hopefully the week will go fast."

"You and me both." I wasn't sure how long the spell would last, but hopefully a week would give it enough time to leave her system.

I sat on the opposite side of the cab and gently pushed her back over to her side every time she got too close. The looks the cab driver was giving me in the rearview mirror were priceless. He thought I'd lost my mind. I'm sure it looked that way. Generally, it wasn't my practice to push away a sexy girl who's trying to get into my pants. Knowing her desire was accentuated by magic didn't make it easier.

"Keep the change." I shoved a couple bills in the driver's hand before helping Casey out of the cab. She unlocked the doors to her building and we stepped into the lobby.

"Want to walk me up?" She cocked her head to one side.

"Yeah, of course." I wasn't leaving her until I knew she was home safely.

"Great, let's go." She took my hand and practically dragged me up the three flights of stairs. Normally, I'd have loved it, but knowing I had to say no really sucked.

We stopped outside her apartment. "I had a great time tonight." She hesitated with a hand on the door. "I don't want to say goodnight though."

"Me either, but we have to. I'll see you for my coffee tomorrow morning."

"You promise?" Her eyes were asking about more than my coffee stop. She wanted assurance I'd be taking her out again.

"Yes. Let's do dinner next time."

She smiled. "Good night, Toby."

"Good night, Casey." I kissed her on the cheek and high-tailed it down the stairs before my chivalrous side lost out to my need to answer the lust rolling off her in waves. Damn my determination to be a gentleman.

"I'm surprised to see you leaving so soon." Eric stepped out of the shadows before I could start looking for him. There was no chance in hell I was leaving her in that state with a bear outside her door.

"Why's that?"

"I saw the way she was looking at you. There was only one thing on her mind."

"I don't take advantage of girls." I kept walking. If he wanted to talk, he'd follow, and the further I could get him from her apartment, the better.

"Was she drunk?"

"Spell from The Sprite House."

He growled. "I hope you didn't set it on her intentionally."

"If I did, would I be leaving her alone in her bed right now?"

"True enough," he grunted. "Are you having her place watched?"

"Yes." I wasn't going to beat around the bush.

"We're watching it too."

"Why?"

"She's important."

I stopped walking. "What does she mean to you?" I didn't believe any of his interest was random.

"She means something to us."

"Real helpful." I played with my keys in my pocket. It was time to show my cards. I needed more information. "You were there that night… I know you were."

He watched the passing traffic, his eyes anywhere but on my face.

I pressed further. "The wolf."

"Wolves. It's the same pack." He finally turned back to look at me. "They keep coming by when she works."

"Why is she being targeted for a kill?"

"We don't know it was for a kill." His hands balled into fists. His anger made him slightly more believable.

"You think they wanted to take her?"

"What is this to you? Do you have some sort of hero's obsession now?" he asked as though I were the one with the problem.

"I saved her because I wasn't going to let some innocent girl get mauled. Where the hell were you? I know you were in there."

"Indisposed." He said the word with distaste.

I grinned. "You almost let her get mauled or kidnapped because you were taking a shit?"

"Obviously, it didn't matter. You just happened to be around."

It didn't take long to figure out what was going on. He was angry at himself for missing his chance to protect her. "Why are you so worried about her?"

"Same reason you are."

"Which is?"

He looked over his shoulder, double checking no one was behind us even though we both would have sensed it. "She's perfect. A fucking wet dream for a mate."

"You're not taking her for a mate." The thought made me sick.

"I'm not?"

"No. Stay away from her." Once again, I felt the urge to transform. I'm sure my eyes were already turning black.

"Chill out, Toby. We're on the same side—for now."

I breathed in and out. Transforming on the street could have some bad repercussions. "How do you see that?"

"We both want her alive and safe."

"And do you have suggestions? Aside from keeping her under constant guard. We're doing that already."

"Nothing concrete yet, but you're thinking exactly what I am."

"Which is?" I turned the corner.

"The attacks relate. Casey being targeted ties in somehow."

I nodded. Not wanting to admit I agreed, but having the same logic moving through my head. "Maybe, but what could an ordinary human have to do with it?"

"I don't know but I plan to find out."

"Does your uncle know?" I already knew the answer, but I had to ask.

"He knows something. He's not talking about it though."

"And the attacks?"

"I don't know. I can't imagine he's behind them. He's not for hurting humans. Especially not women."

"I can agree there. He definitely enjoys them." Marv would probably never settle down with a mate, human or otherwise. Lots of bears mate with their own kind, but more often, they'll pick a human. It's a much larger pool to choose from.

My mind swam with questions, but I knew I wasn't going to get any answers from Eric that night. "Keep me posted, but don't screw with Casey."

"Why? You can't handle the competition?" he taunted.

"You're not competition, but you scare her. I don't want her scared."

"Who would have thought old grandpa killer could have a heart?"

I resisted the urge to punch him. "Shut the hell up." I wasn't proud of what I'd done, but I had no other choice.

"Gladly. If you hear from Casey, tell her I expect to see her at work tomorrow bright and early."

"Not if I have anything to do with it," I grumbled. Who was I kidding? Would I ever tell her to quit her job? And if Eric was telling the truth at all, she was safer there than any other coffee shop. When a Urusus decides he wants a girl as a mate, he doesn't let her get hurt. The same can be said for a Pteron. I stalked off. I had three men watching her place. I'd know if anyone got too close.

Chapter Seven

Casey

For the first time ever, I was late for work. I'd slept straight through my alarm, and I wasn't even fully awake when I left the apartment. I didn't remember much about my first date with Toby the night before except for the amazing coffee and how incredibly attractive he was. I'd had the most sensual dreams ever that night, and I woke up disappointed to find my tiny bed empty. I also had a vague recollection of him asking me out again. Hopefully he'd follow up on the offer. I definitely wanted to see more of him.

I tried to slip into work undetected but, of course, Eric caught me.

"You stood me up." He stood there with his arms crossed, his massive biceps visible underneath his t-shirt.

"I specifically told you I wasn't interested."

"You take playing hard to get to a new level."

"It's because I'm not playing at anything."

He laughed, and it didn't sound forced. In fact, it sounded more natural than any other time I'd heard him. I looked up at him, wondering what had changed. He noticed my perusal and his face immediately went hard. "Get to work. You're staying later to make up for your tardiness."

"Right."

"You're lucky I don't fire your ass."

"Should I be kissing your feet too?"

"Not my feet." He grinned and stalked off. So weird.

"How was it?" Remy asked eagerly when I got back from stowing my stuff in the break room.

"Probably the best coffee date ever."

"I thought you were getting dinner." She set down an Americana for a customer.

"I chickened out on it. I thought coffee was more casual."

"And was it?" She leaned in expectantly.

"Yes, mostly." I really wanted to remember more of the evening. I wondered if the forgetfulness was tied to hitting my head. If so, I really needed to suck it up and see a doctor.

"Mostly?"

"I could barely control myself, I wanted him so bad."

She burst out laughing, scaring the customer who was retrieving her drink.

"Sorry," I apologized to the woman who practically ran out of there. The exchange did nothing to stop Remy's laughter.

"It's not funny. I've never felt that strongly. I even had dreams last night."

"Dreams?"

"Yeah, you know what kind." I wasn't about to go into details about the vivid image of showering with Toby that was probably seared in my brain forever.

"Was there a reason you didn't sleep with him?" Her laughter died down, but it was replaced by a smile that was almost as bad.

"It was our first date." That excuse generally would have covered it, except this time it was the guy putting on the breaks. I refused to read into his reluctance to come in. He had to work.

"Did you take care of it yourself then?" She grinned.

"No." I looked away. That was just something I couldn't do. I didn't view myself as a prude, but a lot of people would.

She shook her head. "Were the dreams satisfying at least?"

"Kind of."

"You might have a chance to live them right now," Remy half yelled.

"What?" I turned around just as Toby walked over to the counter. I groaned. I was positive he'd heard her.

"Hey." He smiled at me, but it was kind of warily. As weird as it sounds, he seemed worried that I was going to attack him or something.

"Hey." I filled a cup with coffee and set it down. "Want anything to go with this?"

"Yeah."

"What?"

"Dinner Saturday night."

A rush of excitement flowed through me. "Didn't I already agree to a second date last night?"

An amused expression crossed his face. "You did, but I wanted to make sure you didn't change your mind in the light of day."

I looked him over. He looked fantastic in the light of day, and although not filled with thoughts of ripping off his clothes, I definitely wanted a second date. "It's still a yes. Saturday sounds great."

"Terrific. I'll give you a call with the details." He grabbed his coffee. "See you soon, Casey."

"Bye." I waved before moving on to the next customer.

***

Mental note: When a rich boy asks you out to dinner, dress up. I'd thought my choice of dark jeans and a black, three-quarter length shirt was perfect for a casual dinner. I was feeling great until I answered my door to find him in a suit.

"Hey." He smiled slightly, looking past me into my apartment.

"Hi. Should I change?" I wasn't going to beat around the bush.

"No. That's okay. I'm just still dressed from work."

"Work on a Saturday?"

His smile grew. "You work on Saturdays."

"Yeah, I work at a coffee shop. Where do you work?"

"Uh, it's a complicated business." He shifted his weight from foot to foot.

"Complicated business? Because that's a detailed description." Evasiveness wasn't an attractive attribute.

He shrugged. "It's not worth the time to explain."

I put a hand on my hip. "I hope you have a better answer than that."

"I work in management." He put a hand in his pocket. "Is that better?"

"Not really, but at least you're trying." I stepped back into my living area. "Do you want to come in?"

"Oh…sure." He seemed reluctant. I was starting to feel self-conscious about Rhett's tiny pad. Maybe it wasn't up to Toby's standard. I wasn't usually so insecure, but I couldn't help but worry even though he'd done nothing to make me feel that money mattered to him. Somehow having him standing there in a suit that probably cost more than the monthly rent made it feel different.

"Are you sure I shouldn't change?"

"Why do you keep asking that?"

"Because I feel underdressed compared to you. Am I going to be appropriately dressed for wherever we're going for dinner?"

"Yeah. Perfectly dressed. I told you it was casual."

"Okay. Then let's go." I grabbed my black purse and followed him out into the hall. After closing and locking the door, we headed to the stairs.

"Have you lived here long?" Toby asked as we walked down the first flight of stairs. Funny, he hadn't asked me anything about that over coffee. It's like we hadn't done anything but flirt on our first date.

"Only a few months. I was in a dorm at NYU before this."

"Oh. Did you graduate?" We reached the final flight.

"No. I only did one semester. I'm going to go back though."

"Sounds like we're in the same boat." He held open the door for me at the bottom and I slipped out with him following.

"Yeah, I heard you were at Princeton."

"You heard right."

He turned left without saying anything. I followed behind him, stepping closer to his side when an ambulance went by. I loved the city, but I hated the constant noise.

"Do you have an aversion to burgers and fries?"

"Burgers and fries? I guess my jeans are okay."

He laughed. It was light and sexy, and it fit him. He needed to do it more often. "I told you."

"I love burgers. Sounds perfect."

"Great. I thought I'd introduce you to my favorite burger joint. It's just a little bit north of here. It's down the block from my place."

"Oh. Cool, but I could have met you there. Why didn't you suggest that?"

"Because I wanted to come by and get you."

"You're all about the vague answers tonight."

"Does that bother you?" He watched me carefully.

"I guess it's better than you not answering at all."

"Are you more straightforward? If I asked you a question, would you answer it head on?"

"Yes," I answered confidently which was pretty brave considering I had no idea what he'd ask.

"Why are you living in that apartment? Why aren't you at NYU?"

"My dad lost his job."

"So he couldn't pay?" He studied my face.

"No. My parents would have probably taken out loans, but I couldn't do that to them." I glanced toward the street. There wasn't a chance I'd put more on their plate.

"So you made the decision to drop out?"

"Yeah, but it's only temporary. I'll go back to school eventually."

"That's really selfless of you." He slipped off his jacket, folding it over his arm.

"They've done enough for me already. I can handle taking a semester off."

"That's a refreshing way of viewing things."

We kept walking, and I was incredibly glad I'd worn my most comfortable boots. Toby's idea of a little bit north was different from my own. I turned the questioning back on him. "So what's your story? Why did you drop out?"

"I guess after your disclosure, I owe you mine?"

"Owe is a strong word, but it would be nice." I smiled, hoping he felt he could trust me enough to tell me something. Anything. The more I talked to him, the more I wanted to know.

"My grandfather died unexpectedly, and I had to step up in the family business."

That was not the answer I was expecting. "Oh. I'm sorry."

His face turned hard, expressionless. "Don't be."

"Oh…you weren't close?"

"Something like that." His expression didn't change, and I decided to drop it.

"Where do you live?" I steered the conversation back to safer territory.

"5th Avenue and 14th."

"Oh, wow. Nice area."

"My place kind of came with the job."

"That's nice. Mine didn't."

He laughed. "So any particular reason you chose to live there then?"

"My cousin offered me a closet."

"A closet?"

"He calls it a bedroom, but it's more of a closet. There's just room enough for a twin bed and my alarm clock. My clothes and everything else are tucked in a corner of the living room."

He half-laughed. "Seriously? That's pretty crazy."

"He only charges me a couple hundred a month, and it beat moving back in with my parents."

"Where are you from?" He slowed down, probably realizing I was struggling to keep up with his brisk pace.

"Long Island."

"What part?"

"Port Jeff."

"That's out east, right?" His hand brushed against mine.

"Not that far east, but eastern Long Island."

"Cool. I went to high school in Westchester, but I spent most of my childhood upstate."

"Oh, that must have been a big move." I'd lived in the same house my whole life until leaving for college, and even then I was only an hour away.

"It was definitely different."

"Which did you like better?" Did he prefer the ritzy burbs or the quiet rural life? I'd never known anything other than suburbia and just recently the city.

"They both had their perks, but I like the city better."

"Do you have any roommates?" He was finally talking, and I wanted to keep it going.

"I live alone, and I like it that way." He said it so simply, like it was the only possible answer. It was the first quasi-personal piece of information he'd given me. I took it eagerly.

"Are you an only child?"

"Digging for more, are you?" He steadied me as a dog ran between us. The owner chased after.

I recovered my footing. "Maybe a little."

"To answer your question, yes. I'm an only child."

"Maybe that's why you like living alone."

He smiled. "What about you? Any brothers or sisters?"

"I have a sister."

"Older, younger?" He looked at me questioningly.

"Older. She's twenty-one."

"Is she still in school?"

"No. Not anymore." Once again, I didn't feel like talking about Vera. Hopefully, he'd get the hint.

"When did you start working at Coffee Heaven?"

Once he got started, the questions didn't stop. "In September, but I only started working full time in January."

"Cool."

"I guess." I smiled up at him as we walked. I checked out the store fronts, wishing I had the money to actually go shopping once in a while.

He held open the door to this hole in the wall looking place.

"You come here a lot?" The burger joint was a hundred and eighty degree change from the swanky coffee house the week before. I wondered why he was changing things up so much. I hoped it had nothing to do with me.

I shook myself for even thinking it. He'd asked me out a second time, hadn't he?

"Yeah. It's quiet and no one bothers me."

"Have you always been this anti-social?"

"No." He followed behind me, holding the door as it closed so it wouldn't slam.

I knew I wasn't getting more of an answer.

We seated ourselves at a little booth with cushions that should have been replaced years before. Toby was definitely right about being dressed just fine. I probably looked over dressed, and I couldn't imagine how Toby felt.

"The burgers are good here?"

"Some of the best."

"Okay, so I guess that's what I should get."

"You're not a vegetarian, are you?" he asked, like he wanted to know whether I had an aversion to puppies and kittens.

"No." Hadn't I already told him I was okay with the cuisine choice? Maybe he expected me to order a veggie burger or something.

"Okay, good."

"Would it matter if I was?" His expression piqued my interest enough that I had to ask.

"No. It would have surprised me though."

"Why's that?"

The waiter came over to take our order so I didn't get my answer right away.

"Two burgers, and you want fries, right?" He turned to me.

"Yes."

"And two orders of fries. Would you like anything to drink? I want a Coke."

"Just a water, please."

The waiter nodded, jotted down the order and walked away.

"You still have to answer." I took out a couple of napkins from the plastic dispenser. The table hadn't been cleaned well, and I couldn't stand looking at the little puddle of ketchup next to my elbow any longer.

"I do?" He grinned. "It just would have meant I was wrong about you. You seem like a red meat eating girl."

"There's a particular look to girls who eat meat?"

"No. You just strike me as someone who likes to eat the good things in life."

I glanced down at my body. "Should I take that as a compliment or a statement about my weight?"

He looked shocked. "A compliment!"

"Okay." I smiled. "Just checking."

"So tell me about your cousin. Is he cool to live with?"

"Most of the time. He's a few years older than me, so we didn't hang out as kids or anything."

"And he's away right now?"

The waiter dropped off our drinks.

"For the next few weeks." I opened my straw and put it in my cup. I was insanely thirsty and took a long sip. "I guess you were listening to our conversation the other night."

"Did I ever pretend I wasn't?" He sipped his Coke.

"No. I just hope you asked me out for the right reasons."

"As compared to the wrong ones?"

"You weren't just trying to be nice, right? Because you knew I was worried about a guy from work bothering me."

"I asked you out because I wanted to. Just like I want to be with you now." He reached over and took my hand.

It was the first physical contact we'd had so far that night. "But you're right to be wary of Eric."

"I am?"

"Yeah. And if you'd feel safer, you're always welcome to stay at my place."

"Excuse me?" I nearly spit out my water.

"Oh. I didn't mean it that way." He looked absolutely horrified by the shock that was probably on my face.

"Then how did you mean it?" I pulled my hand back. Was he really going to be that forward?

"I just mean that if you're scared to stay alone, I have a guest room."

"I'm not scared to stay alone. I just didn't want to go out with him."

"It's okay to be afraid of things."

"I'm not staying over at your place." I looked him straight in the eye as I spoke. "I'm not scared, but is there a reason I should be? What did you mean by I'm right to be wary about Eric?"

"I just know him, and he's a dangerous guy." He looked away slightly.

"Why do I get the sense that you're hiding something from me?" I knew his reluctance to meet my eye wasn't random.

"Because I am." He didn't blink. "I don't want to lie to you. I like you too much to do that."

"Then why would I want to stay in your 'guest room?'" I used air quotes. "If you're keeping things from me, how can I trust you?"

"I don't know, but you should."

Our meals were placed in front of us, and I dug into the juicy burger. Medium rare. My favorite.

We concentrated on our food and didn't talk much. I declined dessert, and before long we got up to leave.

He held open the door, and we walked out into the slightly cool night. "Have you thought any more about staying over?"

"What would have changed my mind?"

"A good meal has been known to clear someone's head."

I laughed. "How about I agree to come over and hang out."

"I'm not asking you so I can get you into bed. I really am trying to look out for you."

"Do you not want me to come over?" I half teased him and half asked out of fear of rejection. Where had all my confidence gone?

"Of course I do." He took my hand. "I'm messing this all up, aren't I?"

"Kinda."

"I'm not trying to push you at all. I'd love to have you come over to hang out, but I have absolutely no expectations for anything else."

"How about coffee?"

"What about it?"

"Can we have some at your apartment? You do own a coffee maker, don't you?"

He chuckled. "Of course, I own a coffee maker."

"Just checking."

He held my hand as we walked down the street.

I pulled out my phone and texted Remy.

I'm going back to Toby's place.

Our unofficial rule from first semester was that you always text to say you were going to a guy's place. That way, if you went missing, they'd know the first place to look. It isn't the most foolproof method, but it's something.

Ok. I'm calling if I don't hear from you by midnight.

Thanks.

"Who are you texting?" Toby glanced over.

"A friend." No need to tell him who.

"Oh. That way they'll know where to find your body."

I gasped. "Is that supposed to be a joke?"

He gave me a wry grin. "Of course."

"I think you're rusty." My body relaxed slightly. I guess that's what you'd call a straight-faced delivery.

We stopped in front of a fairly modern looking building. A uniformed doorman opened the door. "Good evening, Mr. Welsh."

Toby nodded. "Hi, Cody." He led the way to an elevator and hit the button for the top floor as soon as I stepped in. "You have the top floor? Like the penthouse?"

"Yeah. It's a nice perk."

After what felt like an insanely long time of standing silent in the elevator, the doors opened and he went right over to his apartment.

He unlocked the door and I walked in. "I thought these places only existed in movies." I headed straight through his living room to the floor to ceiling windows.

"The view's pretty nice."

"Pretty nice? Try incredible."

He smiled. "I've seen better."

"I need to start moving in the circles you're in," I mumbled.

"Trust me, you don't want to."

I turned around. He'd stopped a few feet behind me and was looking out. "Want to make that coffee?"

"Oh, yeah, sure." He walked into a modern kitchen that was bigger than my apartment. The stainless steel appliances fit well with the light wood cabinets and travertine tile floor.

"Do you cook?" I hoped this gorgeous place wasn't wasted on a guy who couldn't make eggs.

"I'm learning."

"Learning?"

"I didn't know how a few months ago, but I'm making do."

"Oh, okay." That was something.

"Do you cook?" He scooped coffee beans into a grinder.

"Yeah. I love cooking."

"Nice to know some girls still like to." He pushed down on the lid of the grinder.

I waited for the noise to stop. "What's that mean?"

"Oh. Just that my ex hated cooking. She told me whatever guy she married would have to do it for her." He picked up the grinder and dumped the ground coffee into the filter.

"Allie?" I covered my mouth with my hand. I hadn't meant to say it out loud.

"Yeah. Did Jess tell you about her?" He poured in the water and turned the coffee machine on.

I tried to make my interest sound as innocent as possible. "She mentioned they were friends."

"Yeah. She broke my heart into about a million pieces, but you gotta move on, right?"

Jess seemed so convinced he'd dumped Allie, but he didn't seem to see it that way. "I've had a bad breakup before. They're not fun."

"How long did it take to get over the guy?"

"A few months."

"Good to know." He pulled down two large, green coffee mugs.

"I might be pushing my luck, but do you have anything sweet?"

"Sweet? I thought you didn't want dessert?"

"I didn't, but I do now."

He walked over to a cabinet and pulled out a box of brownie mix. "Want to make these?"

"Brownies? You want to bake brownies?"

He put the box down on the counter. "You're the one who said you wanted dessert. I'm just trying to be a good host."

I laughed. "I never imagined we'd be making brownies tonight, but why not?"

"I'll get a bowl."

I watched as he pulled out a large glass mixing bowl and preheated the oven. The situation should have been completely awkward, but it wasn't. It was natural in a weird way.

I cracked the eggs while he poured in the oil and water. I grabbed a spoon and started mixing before he could. "Why don't you get our coffee?"

"How do you like yours?"

"Drowned in milk." I finished the last few strokes and set the bowl aside.

"Really? I'd have thought you liked it black."

"Why? Because you do?" I hunted down a pan and cooking spray.

"No. You just seem like a black coffee kind of person."

"First I'm a red meat eating girl and now a black coffee drinker?" I gave him a disbelieving look. "I don't like sugar in it though."

"Okay…so I was half right."

"I suppose you could look at it that way."

He grabbed the bowl and poured the batter in. "Do you want to lick the spoon?"

"I hope you're referring to licking brownie batter."

"I assure you, I've never referred to my dick as a spoon before."

I coughed.

"If you're going to throw it, you need to be able to take it." Aside from the twinkle in his eye, he looked completely serious.

I regained my composure. "Give me the spoon."

He handed it over, finally letting a smile slip out.

"Do you stay away from raw batter?"

"No, but I prefer it straight from the bowl." He ran a finger along the inside of the bowl and licked the batter off his finger.

"Okay, let's wash this stuff so we can get rid of all these sexual innuendos."

"That's probably a good idea." He took the spoon from me and brought both over to his double sink.

"Your kitchen is bigger than my apartment." I grabbed my cup of coffee and took a seat at the island.

He finished washing the dishes and set them aside. "I'm well aware. I've been there."

"That's right. You have."

He took a seat next to me. "I bet you're wondering what I know about Eric."

"Maybe a little." I cautiously sipped the hot coffee. No amount of milk could cool it down that fast.

"He's dangerous."

"Dangerous? I admit he's obnoxious, but dangerous seems a little bit much."

"He's dangerous." Toby rested his hand on the counter. "Can I ask you a question now?"

"Sure."

"Why did you agree to go out with me last week? You asked me what motive I had, what about you?"

"Because you asked me." I'm sure I blushed.

"Somehow I doubt you're that hard up for a date."

"What does hard up have to do with it?" I attempted another sip.

"Are you going to pretend you've been waiting for me to ask you out?"

I laughed nervously. "Not waiting, but I've never been opposed to it."

"Does that mean you aren't that friendly to all your customers?" He finished off his coffee.

"I'm always friendly, but I try harder with you."

"Try harder?" He drew little circles on the counter with his fingers. Either it was a nervous habit, or he was really bored. I hoped it was the former.

"You didn't exactly make it easy. You never even asked my name."

"Because I knew it. I heard you talking to your friend the first time I came in."

"Really?"

He moved his hand closer to where mine rested on the countertop. "Really."

"What else did you know about me?" I sipped my coffee again while trying to hide the excitement I felt that the interest hadn't been completely one-sided.

"That you were cute and perky and were the bright spot of my day." He glanced down into his empty cup.

"The bright spot of your day?" His words got me—there was something so genuine about them.

"I'm not elaborating. I've embarrassed myself enough."

"You haven't embarrassed yourself." Wow. Could he be any cuter? I thought rich guys who lived in penthouses were supposed to be alpha male assholes.

"You need to stay away from Eric."

"That's not really possible, and you still haven't told me why he's dangerous." I allowed the subject change, considering how honest he'd been with me.

"I can't tell you the details, but he can seriously hurt you."

"Does he have a history of abuse? Do you know him from somewhere?"

"Business."

"Ooh, the mysterious business again."

He chuckled. "Trust me. You don't want to know about it."

"I do, but that doesn't mean you're going to tell me."

"Not tonight."

I got my first full sip in. I enjoyed the warmth in the cool kitchen. "But maybe another time?"

He shrugged. "Maybe."

"I have to work with Eric. I can't completely stay away from him."

"You could always quit your job."

"Not all of us have family businesses to fall back on." I couldn't hide the iciness in my voice.

"At least be careful. You don't want his attention."

"I already have it."

"Maybe you shouldn't look so good at work."

"Excuse me?" I nearly choked on my coffee.

"Even if Eric was just a regular guy, he'd still have trouble resisting you."

"You make it sound like I dress like a tramp…"

"That's not what I'm saying. You just look good."

"You're not making any sense." I dared to take another sip. Hopefully he wouldn't shock me with a crazy statement again.

"I'm trying to say I get why he's interested. You'd be a hard girl to work with and not hit on." He got up and refilled his coffee cup.

"You really are out of practice," I mumbled.

"Out of practice?"

He'd heard that? "Yeah…just something Emmett mentioned."

"I tend to be a bit of a loner now."

"Is this all because of your breakup?"

"Partly. It's not something I'm in the mood to talk about."

"Then what do you want to talk about?" I pushed up the sleeves of my shirt. Three sips in and I'd gone from cold to hot.

"Drinking something stronger than coffee."

"What do you have in mind?" I took another sip.

"Should I open a bottle of wine?"

My brain said no. Drinking a bottle of wine with a guy at his place would only lead to one thing, but my body said something altogether different. My body won out. "Sounds good."

"Great. Are you into Barolo at all?"

"Yeah, definitely." I knew nothing about wine, but it sounded good.

"Great."

Two hours, and two glasses of wine later, I was curled up on the couch and laughing with him. We talked about nothing and everything and took in the view. The wine tasted heavenly, and went perfectly with the gooey brownies, but it also made me tired, and the thought of going home sounded anything but appealing. My head was swimming. "Is that guest room option still available?

"Yeah, of course." He smiled, and I let out a sigh of relief. Part of me worried he'd suggested the wine for a less than noble reason, but maybe he did just want to hang out.

"Thanks."

"I knew you'd change your mind." He adjusted his arm behind me.

"Did you?"

"Yeah. If not now, when you saw the room."

"Is it nice?"

"Very. Not quite the same view as my room, but I bet it beats your closet."

I laughed. "I'm sure it does. I can't believe I'm doing this."

"Doing what?"

"Willingly staying in a guy's guest room."

"I'd hope you wouldn't do it unwillingly."

"You know what I mean."

"Yeah, I do." He brushed some hair away from my face. "I'm not going to hurt you, Casey. I'm not going to pretend I'm the safest guy for you to be around, but I won't let anything happen to you."

"Is that your way of saying you're dangerous too?"

"Possibly."

"You're so mysterious." I pulled my leg up on the couch.

"Is that good or bad?"

"Both. It's frustrating, but also kind of sexy." At the moment, the sexy part was winning out.

"Sexy, huh?" He smiled. "I'll take that."

"What about me?"

"What about you?" He scooted a little closer.

"Am I sexy?" The wine made me far braver than I'd normally be.

"Sexy enough that I'd much rather be offering my bed than the guest room."

"Maybe next time," I said flirtatiously.

"Are you trying to kill me here?"

"Nope. That's your job. You're the one worried about someone finding my body."

He smiled. "Want me to show you your room?"

"It's my room now?"

"It is anytime you want it." He got up and set aside his empty glass. I did the same and followed him out of the living room.

He paused in front of a door. "If you need anything, I'm right down the hall, but you should have mostly everything in there."

"Thanks. I appreciate it."

"I appreciate your company." He leaned over and kissed my cheek. "Goodnight, Casey."

I touched my cheek where his lips had made contact, and pushed open the door.

Chapter Eight

Toby

Was I an idiot? Did I really just give up my second opportunity to spend the night with her? This time, I couldn't figure out what she wanted, but she seemed to want her own space. Hopefully, her playful promise of a next time was real. I wasn't sure how many more of these nights my body could handle. I didn't have time to worry about it long. As soon as the guest room door clicked closed, my phone rang.

"Toby." Tim's voice broke through the line immediately. "Two more bodies in Jersey."

"Fuck." I leaned my head against the wall. "I have to call him, don't I?"

"Yes. I'm sure he's figured it out already, but you need to do it."

"All right." I hung up on Tim and made it down the hall to my office. Much smaller than the one I had at work,it fit me better. I preferred the black desk to the mahogany one across town.

I hesitated with my phone long enough to scroll through the names. Allie's name was still on top. I needed to change that. Deleting her didn't feel right, but I could add in her last name—Davis. The problem was that her name would be changing soon, to Laurent. My human ex-girlfriend becoming the queen of a supernatural society should have seemed strange, but it wasn't anymore. I'd finally accepted it—mostly.

I found Levi's number and made myself press connect.

"Took you long enough." Levi answered with a cockiness that pissed me off.

"I thought we had it under control." I spun my chair so I could gaze out at the night.

"I'm giving you the benefit of the doubt, but we can't let this continue. How many bodies is it now? Nearing twenty?"

"Something like that." It was twenty-two.

"What do you know?" I heard a muffled voice. He wasn't alone. I wondered if he was at home in bed with Allie. I quickly cleared that thought from my head.

"Bears and wolves."

"Tell me something I don't already know," he snapped. He tried to act so calm and collected, but he was freaking out. For all his arrogance, he was new to the job too.

"Close to ten groups confirmed."

"I figured that much. This wasn't one pack and clan. They want attention, and we can't let them get it."

"You've been contacted, haven't you?"

"Yeah. The president's already called." He said it so nonchalantly, like it was a daily activity to take a call from the President of the United States.

"You told him everything was under control?"

"Of course. Now let's get it under control. It's starting in New York, but we all know it's not staying there."

"What do you want me to do? Full on investigation with interrogations?"

"I'm sending someone up."

"You don't have to." I leaned back in my chair. I didn't need any of Laurent's men.

"Jared's the best we have."

"Jared Florence?" I didn't know the guy well, but I knew of him. He was Levi's childhood friend and notoriously ruthless.

"He's head of security now."

"I know. I was at your coronation…" I'd flown down both out of obligation and to make myself watch Allie move on. Watching your ex take her place as another man's queen helps give you some closure.

"He'll be there soon."

"If that's what you want."

"It is."

"How is she?" I forced the question out. I needed to know.

"Allie's good, really good."

"Great." I meant it. Our messed up history aside, I cared about her. I wanted her happy whether it was with me or not.

"I'll tell her you said hi."

Once again, I wondered if she was listening to his end of the call. "Even though I didn't say it?"

"You thought it."

"I wasn't aware you could read minds, Laurent." Respect wasn't something I worried about with Levi. Sooner or later, his appreciation for saving Allie would wear off, and I'd have to drop the attitude. But until then, I wasn't walking on egg shells for him.

"It doesn't take mind reading. I'll get a report from Jared soon." He hung up.

"Fantastic." I closed my eyes again, trying to fight off the headache I knew was coming.

The knock on the door was light, tentative even.

"Come in." I sat up straighter. I'd been so caught up in my conversation with Levi that I had almost forgotten Casey was there.

"Hey." She had her brown hair pulled up in a bun. It reminded me of the morning after I'd taken care of the wolf for her. She looked gorgeous with her hair down, but there was something 'girl next door' hot about when she wore it up.

"Hey. Is everything okay?" I hoped she hadn't changed her mind about staying. Momentary forgetfulness didn't mean I didn't want her there. Having her under my roof felt right. Even if I'd have much preferred to have her in my bed.

"I have a favor to ask." She blushed slightly, making me both curious and excited about what she was going to ask.

"Sure."

"Can I borrow something to sleep in?"

"Oh, yeah. Like a t-shirt and shorts?" I probably should have thought to offer earlier. She wasn't going to sleep in jeans.

"That would work."

I got out from behind my desk and walked down the hall to my room. She followed closely behind me until I walked through the doorway. She hesitated in the hall.

"Is that the view you were talking about?" She pointed at my floor to ceiling windows.

"Yeah. It's a nice way to wake up."

"I'm sure."

I pulled out a clean pair of basketball shorts and a white t-shirt. "They're going to be big, but it's all I have."

"That's all right." She smiled, walking into my room to take the clothing from me. I liked having her in there. I'd imagined it quite a few times. Of course, in my fantasies she wasn't coming in to get more clothing, she was taking hers off.

I didn't want her to leave. I wanted her to spend the night in my bed, but I knew that wasn't an option. "Do you need anything else? I'm pretty sure there's toothpaste and an extra toothbrush and stuff in your bathroom."

"Pretty sure? You didn't stock the place yourself?"

I shook my head. "Not exactly. One of my assistants did it."

"What else do your assistants do for you?" she mumbled, probably assuming I couldn't hear.

I decided to spare her the embarrassment of answering that no, I don't screw my employees.

"Well, thanks. I'll see you in the morning." She half waved before disappearing through the doorway.

I slumped down on the end of the bed, trying to ignore the urge to beg her to come back.

Chapter Nine

Jared

"Come on, you can do better than that!" Yelling at the queen would get most people in trouble, but it was the only way to get her ass moving when we worked out together. I'd been training Allie for months, and she was doing incredibly well, but she was still human.

She groaned. "I'm exhausted."

"Suck it up. We've got another thirty minutes to go."

"I'm taking a break." She picked up her blue water bottle and started to drink.

I tried to hide my grin. She was doing amazing, but I couldn't tell her that. The harder I pushed her, the better she did.

My phone vibrated in my pocket. I picked up immediately when Levi's office number showed up on my screen. He spent as little time in that basement room as possible. "Hey, man."

Levi's voice replied immediately. "We've got problems. Get down here now."

"Gotcha." Levi rarely ordered me around. If he did, it was for a good reason.

"Drop Allie off at the house and get Owen."

"I'm on it." I hung up, knowing that he'd just get pissed if I wasted more time. Having your best friend turn into your boss and the king complicates things, but I wouldn't have traded my position for anything. I always thought it would go to my brother, but he fucked up big time and was currently rotting away in a prison cell.

"Looks like you get off easy today, Princess." She may have been queen, but I still called her princess. It fit better and she always got annoyed when I called her it.

"Was that Levi?" Her face seemed to light up now when she asked about him. Those two were seriously in love.

"Yeah. I'll take you home."

After dropping Allie off at their ridiculously huge house, I ran by my place to get Owen. He'd just returned from his own workout.

"Sounds like shit's hit the fan. Let's go." I pulled off my t-shirt and headed to the porch. The quickest way to travel at night was flying. I didn't look behind me to check that Owen was following. He'd get there eventually.

Flying was like a breath of fresh air to me. I couldn't go a day without it. Some Pterons resist the urge, trying to blend in, but I didn't bother. I usually only flew during night time hours, but with our limited need for sleep, that still gave me plenty of airtime. I reluctantly landed all too soon and pulled on my t-shirt. Owen did the same next to me.

We walked into the lobby of the Crescent City Hotel. The same punk bell boy kid who always worked stepped out of the way as we walked through. I wondered if he had any clue what the basement housed. Probably not. Otherwise, he'd be a hell of a lot more afraid of me.

I slid the security card into the elevator. That little card would allow us access to the basement level. Most people had no clue about the existence of the lower level considering basements were rare in a city built below sea level. We preferred to keep it that way. The fewer people who knew our secrets, the better.

A human wouldn't have been able to see anything when they stepped off the elevator car, but Owen and I could see perfectly. One of the perks of being a Pteron was near perfect night vision.

We walked down the marble hallway. As a kid, I always imagined I'd be coming down on official business. The reality wasn't quite as awesome as I imagined, mostly because there weren't any girls involved, but it still felt good.

I knocked on Levi's office, more out of habit from when it belonged to his father than for any real attempt at respect. Levi and I went too far back as friends for that.

"Come in." Levi sounded stressed. That wasn't a good sign. He could usually hold it together pretty well. I already had an idea what the call was about, but I wasn't positive.

Owen pushed open the door. Levi was seated in his chair behind the heavy wooden desk that took up half the room. For a king's office, it wasn't particularly large or fancy. Maybe the idea was to make the office unappealing so you spent as little time inside as possible.

"All hell is breaking out in New York." Levi didn't wait a beat.

"Meaning?"

"Meaning the body count is rising, the human powers that be want us to fix it—fast."

"Didn't you put Allie's ex in charge there? Isn't this his problem?" I didn't really know Toby, but anyone who got in Levi's way was on my shit list. Call it protective instinct.

"He answers to me, but New York is still my territory." The look he gave me made it clear he was still annoyed that Allie had given away California in a desperate and stupid attempt to save her friends. He acted like he didn't care, but giving up power—no matter how small—sucks.

"Do you need me to go up there?" Maybe I'd get my vacation after all. I hadn't been to New York City in ages.

"Yes. Can you head up tonight? I told Toby we're stepping in."

"Does Allie know?"

"Not yet. I'll have to tell her though. She's been glued to the news."

"Her parents are okay?" Surprisingly enough, I actually cared.

"Yeah. They're always under watch."

"Does she know that?" Allie had a short fuse when it came to Levi withholding information from her. He tended to do that a lot.

"Yes. It was actually her idea." He straightened up in his seat.

"Nice. Maybe she is learning."

"You'll check things out and report back to me?"

"Definitely. Do you still have that place on Central Park for me to stay in?"

He nodded and tossed the keys. "Yeah. I'm not getting rid of that apartment anytime soon."

"Cool." My trip was sounding better and better. Levi's place on the Upper West Side was sweet.

"Don't do anything stupid, Jared. Concentrate on the job."

"Would I ever do something stupid?"

"Yes, when it involves a blonde who's stacked."

"I guess I'll have to stay away from the blondes then. I'll call you as soon as I have news."

"Good. We need to crush these assholes fast. They're only doing this because they think I'm weak. Let's show them how wrong they are."

"Now that sounds like Levi." Owen laughed.

"Owen, I need you to stay around. I'm sure these northern rebels aren't working alone. We need to figure out how to stop it before it starts down here."

"Have fun you two." I strode out of Levi's office feeling pretty darn good. It was time to show Levi he'd picked the right security chief.

Chapter Ten

Toby

My alarm went off at seven a.m. I groaned, thinking back on the days when the weekend meant sleeping in. Not anymore. I dragged myself out of bed and into the shower. By the time I got out, I'd already missed two calls from Tim. I had to get moving.

I paused outside the guestroom, feeling a bit like a creeper as I listened to her breathe. She was still sleeping. I walked into the kitchen, made a pot of coffee and left a quick note.

I'll be back in a few hours. Feel free to make anything. I'll walk you home.

-Toby

I didn't bother to pour myself a cup. I was already running late. Besides, I was heading to a meeting at a coffee house. It wasn't exactly neutral territory, but I'd learned that sometimes you have to go to your adversaries to get things done.

I pushed open the doors of Coffee Heaven without the usual anticipation. The only reason I went there was currently sleeping in my apartment. The thought made me wish she were in a different bed—the one I'd just left. But then again, would I have been able to make myself leave if that were the case? It had been months since I'd been with a girl, and I knew that Casey was the type you wanted just as much in the morning as you did at night.

"Toby. How nice of you to visit us this morning." Marv, a hulking figure, turned to look at me. I'd come to view him as an ally since being brought into the fold by my grandfather, but now I had to doubt every interaction.

"Let's get right to business." I was in a hurry. I actually had a reason to get home. But I wasn't leaving without answers.

"And what kind of business is that?" Marv shot me a cocky grin. "I haven't had the pleasure of meeting with you lately."

"Cut the crap. I know you're behind the attacks."

"Me?" He put a hand to his chest in mock innocence.

"Enough of the bull shit." I strode toward him.

"Eric? Do you know what Toby is referring to?" He called to his nephew, the second reason I was anxious for the meeting.

"No. No, I don't."

I reached out and pulled Marv toward me by his collar and lifted him off the ground. My grandfather had taught me the art of intimidation. "Don't fuck with me. What role do you have in this?"

"Let go of me." He struggled, but I didn't let him go. Six months before, I'd have been scared shitless at what I was doing. By that point, it was just part of a day's work.

"Why the attacks?" I had to have answers.

"You're vulnerable."

"What did you just say?" I shook him a little harder. I wasn't surprised that his nephew didn't step in. Assaulting me would be a big mistake.

"The Pterons are weak. You can't hold out on top forever."

"So attacking humans is the solution?" I could feel my body trying to transform, anger was an easy trigger. If you didn't fight it, it could happen in the worst situations. This wasn't one of them—well, it would have been for Marv. I doubt he would have ever walked again.

"They're getting attention..."

"They? Are you going to claim you're not part of it?"

He attempted to shake his head despite his precarious situation. "I'm not. I'm just pretending. The others think I'm going along with it, but I'm not. We're staying out of it."

I let go and he fell back into his chair. "Pretending? You expect me to believe that?"

"Yes. And you can't prove anything to the contrary."

He had me there. My cousins hadn't managed to get anything more than rumors. "If I find out you did..."

"I know." He fixed his collar. "Don't waste your breath."

"You're going to find out what's going on." I may have dropped him, but my gaze hadn't left his face. Sometimes a look can be a hell of a lot more intimidating than touch.

"What?"

"If you're pretending, this new assignment shouldn't be hard. Get dirty and find out."

"Is that an order?"

"Yes."

He nodded, any hint of his earlier joking gone. "Is that all?"

"From you. Eric's next."

"He's had nothing to do with this." Marv quickly jumped to his defense. Did the ruthless man actually have a soft spot for his sister's kid?

"It's about a different matter." I strode out the front door.

Eric followed me. "I don't have anything new, except she didn't come home last night."

"And I'm sure you know where she slept instead." Maybe I should have been trying to protect her reputation, but Eric needed to back off.

"Not Mr. Chivalrous anymore?"

"I am, but she'll hopefully be staying over more often now."

"I'm still posting a watch, and you need to be careful."

"I will be." Something was off. He didn't seem nearly as jealous as he should have. Bears are prone to uncontrolled jealousy. "What aren't you telling me?"

"Just take care of her. She's important."

"There's more."

"Isn't there always?" He walked back inside.

I wasn't sure what to make of Eric's calm appearance, but I didn't stop to worry about it. There was something much more pressing and appealing waiting for me back home.

Chapter Eleven

Casey

The sheets must have been at least eight hundred-thread count. I wrapped myself up in the blue top sheet, feeling absolutely no desire to get out of bed. If the guest sheets were nice, what were Toby's like? I shook myself. I was not allowed to fantasize about sleeping with a guy just to enjoy nice sheets. Or a nice view. I'd seen his windows the night before, and I wouldn't mind waking up to that view. I wouldn't mind waking up every morning in the guest room either. It definitely beat my closet.

Light spilled in through a small slit in one of the blinds. That was something else my closet lacked, a window. If I'd had the energy, I would have gotten up to pull the blinds up further. I love waking up to natural light, and I missed it every day at Rhett's apartment.

I glanced at the clock. Eight thirty a.m. It had been a fabulous night in luxury land, but it was morning and time to go home. Too bad Toby wasn't looking for a roommate. I would have answered that ad. I'm sure plenty of girls would—and not just as a platonic roommate. I gave myself a few minutes to think about him. Even through his shirts, I could tell his body was the perfect mix of lean and muscular. I wondered what his chest would feel like under my hand, what his lips would feel like on mine. I always pictured he'd be the gentle kind of guy, but the hint of his personality I'd gotten the night before made me wonder if there was something much more primal underneath.

I pushed the thoughts away. There was no reason to go there. Especially not when I was sleeping in a bed down the hall from his.

I needed to wake up, but maybe a few minutes more of comfort wouldn't hurt. I curled up.

Bam. Bam. I sat up with a start. What the heck was that?

Bam. Bam. Bam. The noise repeated, and I realized it was someone pounding on the front door.

I laid back down, putting the pillow—wrapped in a super soft pillow case, might I add—over my head.

The insistent banging wouldn't stop. I rolled over, waiting for Toby to take care of whoever was there. Who had guests that early on a Sunday morning? Especially ones that rude.

The pounding continued. And continued.

Where the heck was Toby? He had to hear it unless his room was soundproof or something.

Boom. Boom.

Maybe it was stupidity, but I reluctantly pulled myself out of the luxurious sheets, ran a hand through my rumpled hair and looked for Toby. I didn't bother to brush my teeth, but then again, I didn't plan on him getting too close to my mouth.

The door to Toby's room was open, but he wasn't there. His bed was unmade, and he'd left some discarded clothes on the floor. His office was just as empty.

I searched around for a weapon. Anything I could use to protect myself. Who knew who was on the other side? I had a choice. I could sit tight and wait for whoever it was to either go away or break down the door. Or, I could answer it. The thought of someone breaking down the door while I huddled in the corner is what made the decision. I was going to meet whoever it was head on—even if it was while I was holding a lamp.

I mustered the most confident voice possible. "Whoever you are, Toby isn't home."

"Could you open the door?" a male voice asked. The voice was deep and kind of sexy. I wondered if the owner of the voice matched it. Not to mention, I hoped the owner of the voice wasn't insane.

"Who are you?"

He sighed, like my even asking the question was ridiculous. "I'm here on business. I need to talk to Toby."

"He's not here."

"I'm not going away until you open the door."

"People know I'm here. If you kill me, you won't get away with it."

He laughed. "I'm not going to kill you."

"How do I know that?"

"Because I gave my name to the doorman, I've been caught on no less than six surveillance cameras on the way up here, and I don't generally go around killing people. Especially not girls."

"Why are you less likely to kill girls?"

"Because I like them. A lot."

I slowly opened the door and my jaw dropped. Standing there was a shirtless guy with a body that couldn't be real. Hard. Muscular. Perfect. That's the way I'd describe his chest. He had abs that would make underwear models jealous. My eyes zeroed in on a few beads of sweat making a descent down his chest. When they reached his stomach, I forced my eyes up to his face.

He grinned. "So you're why Toby isn't getting the job done."

"What?" I asked, forcing my eyes to stop looking at his chiseled abs.

"You'd distract me too." He didn't bother to hide his appraisal.

I looked down and crossed my arms. I met his eyes again and was met by an expression of humor and want that nearly melted me.

"I'm just staying here." I felt the need to explain myself. If not for my sake or dignity, for Toby's. I promised myself it wasn't because I wanted this sexy guy to know I was single.

"Staying here, huh?" He smiled. "Well, you can stay at my place anytime."

"Do you live around here?" His wider grin made me regret the words. "I'm just wondering. Not because I want to stay with you."

"I'm from New Orleans, but I have a place here too—at least I'm borrowing it."

"Oh. Well, Toby isn't here."

"You already said that." He stepped into the apartment. "Know where he is?"

"No. I don't." I took a few steps back.

He matched my movements, ending up just as close to me as he was before. "No kiss goodbye this morning?"

"That would have been hard since I was in the guest room." I put a hand on my hip. Sexy or not, I wasn't going to let this guy get to me.

"Guest room? Likely."

I could feel my blood boiling. How was he getting under my skin so easily? "It's true. If you'll excuse me, I need to get my stuff and go home."

"Are you going to wear that?" He gestured to my outfit, and that's when I remembered what I was sleeping in.

I willed myself not to blush, but I could practically feel the blood rushing to my face.

"I'm guessing those are the guest pajamas, huh?"

"I just borrowed them… Wait, why am I bothering to explain myself to you?"

"I don't know, you tell me." He took another step toward me.

"I know the kind of guy you are."

"You do? Please, tell me. I can't wait to hear this assessment."

"You're arrogant, pig headed, and you think a girl's just going to fall to her knees if you take your shirt off…" To my credit, I was still standing. "Speaking of which, why is your shirt off?"

He smirked. "Why do you think it's off? Since apparently you're the expert on guys like me. I'm going to ignore the fall to their knees comment. You look cute when you blush, but it might push you over the edge."

"I'm sure there's a reason for it." I crossed my arms, wishing I were in my own clothes and wishing he hadn't made me think about falling to my knees around him.

That just made me wonder if his lower half was as impressive as his top.

"There is. Maybe I'll tell you about it sometime." As if he could read my thoughts, he adjusted the waist of his jeans.

"Not likely. Is there a reason you're still here even though I told you Toby's out?"

"Yes. He wasn't in his office either. I need to find him."

"I won't be able to help you there."

"But you might be able to help me in other ways?" He smirked again, and I had a feeling those kind of lines had worked for him before.

"Could you just leave?"

"I suppose I could. Is that what you want?"

I nodded.

"Maybe I'll see you around again. I think I missed your name though."

"You didn't miss it. I never told you."

"Oh, I see. I'm Jared." He held out his hand like he wanted to shake. I resisted the urge to take it, to find out what his touch felt like.

"If you're going to be that way." He flashed me another smile before walking out the door. "See you around, sleep over girl."

I stepped back and closed the door behind him, a mix of relief yet surprise that he'd left so easily. I thought I would have to kick him out.

I walked back into the guest room and threw on my clothes from the night before. I wanted to try a shower that actually had hot water, but knowing my luck, Jared would be back. Jared. I liked the way the name felt rolling off my tongue.

I grabbed my purse and started to walk out, but then I realized I'd be leaving the door unlocked. I sighed before picking up my phone and calling Toby.

He answered immediately. "Casey? You're up?"

"Hey. Yeah…you had a visitor."

"A visitor? Who? Are you okay?" His voice bordered on panic.

"His name was Jared. He said he had business to discuss with you or something."

"Jared? Jared Florence." Toby groaned. "He didn't bother you, did he?"

"Define bother."

"I'll take that as a no then. You'd know if he did. I'm on my way home. Give me two minutes." He hung up.

I took a seat on his huge sectional and looked out at the city. Growing up in the suburbs, I always dreamed of living in New York City, but the reality of it wasn't as great as I imagined. I was starting to wonder if it was worth it. My experience would have been different if I'd lived in a place like Toby's rather than a closet.

I got up and walked into the kitchen, figuring that as long as I was waiting around, I might as well make coffee. He'd evidently made it for me and left a note.

I poured two cups, assuming Toby would want one.

I heard the door open. "Hey."

"Good morning," I called from the kitchen.

Toby sat down at the island. He was dressed in a suit again. "I'm sorry about Jared. I should have made sure he knew not to come by."

"Were you at church?" I handed him his cup of coffee.

"Church?"

"You're pretty dressed up for a Sunday morning."

"Oh, I had a meeting."

"A meeting this early on a Sunday?"

"Yeah…thanks for the coffee." He lifted up his cup.

"All I did was pour it, you're the one who made it. And was the meeting about anything interesting, at least?" I fished for information. Between the morning meeting, the shirtless guy at the door, and all his talk about Eric, his mysteriousness was becoming more frustrating.

He opened his mouth, and then closed it. Like he was weighing the pros and cons of telling me something. "The meeting was actually with your boss."

"My boss?"

"Yeah. With Marv. Eric was there too."

"What?" I set down my coffee hard enough to spill a little bit of it. "Tell me everything, right now."

"I can't tell you everything."

"You met with my boss without my permission."

"Your permission? Do you think the meeting was about you?"

"Of course, I do. What else would it be?" I seethed. He had completely overstepped his bounds.

"I already told you I do business with them…it had nothing to do with you—at first."

"At first?" I leaned on the counter.

"I did have a few choice words with Eric…"

"What was the first part of the meeting about?"

"I can't tell you."

"You can't or you won't?"

"A little of both." He pulled out the stool next to him. It was the same one I'd sat on the night before. "But if you sit down, I can tell you about the parts that involve you."

I sat, not because he told me to, but because I already wanted to. "Start talking."

"Eric claims he was trying to protect you too."

"Protect me?"

"Has anything strange happened to you lately?"

"Strange?"

"Yes. Anything out of the ordinary?"

Like almost being mauled by a giant wolf. "No."

"Come on, Casey. Be honest with me." His eyes implored me to share.

"Yes," I reluctantly admitted. It was harder to do than you'd think. It meant admitting I was either losing my mind or a witness to something terrifying.

"Then you probably already know that there are some crazy things happening around here."

"Do you know what happened to me?" I strongly suspected what his answer would be.

"Yes."

I took a chance that he was being honest and that we were on the same page. "And was there actually a wolf?"

"Yes, but it wasn't a random wolf acting alone."

I wanted to tell him about the guy with wings, but then he'd just think I was crazy. That part couldn't have been real. "How could a wolf act with someone else? Like someone trained him and sent him after me?"

He looked away. "I can't say much else. It's just that you're being targeted, and I don't know why."

"Targeted?"

"Eric doesn't think that the wolf was trying to hurt you."

"Not hurt me? Why else would it have cornered me and then lunged for me."

"Eric didn't get outside in time, but he says it wasn't the first time he's sensed the wolf. He'd seen wolves around weeks before the attacks started."

"The attacks? The ones in the parks?" The news reports were becoming more and more frequent, but they never seemed to have any new information to share.

"And out in Jersey."

"Putting aside the fact that giant wolves are attacking people, why has a wolf been hanging around the coffee shop? And why didn't it want to kill me? The others were killed."

"It wants you for something…I guess. And it's not just wolves behind the attacks. It's also bears."

"Bears? There are bears roaming the streets of New York now?" I gave him a skeptical look. If I hadn't seen the wolf with my own eyes, I wouldn't have believed a word of it.

"Yes, but the bottom line is you're being targeted. I don't know by who exactly or why, but you are."

"And Eric wants to protect me? I thought he was trying to sleep with me." I finally sat back. "My mistake."

"He does want to sleep with you, hence the push to protect you. Or so he says."

"Is that why you're helping me?"

He paled. "Not the only reason."

Did he actually say that?

"Don't look so surprised. Like I said, it's not the only reason. I care about you, and I'm not going to let you get hurt. That's all that matters."

I processed the new information. So far, Toby hadn't done anything to make me doubt him, but giant wolves and bears attacking the city were hard to believe. I needed time to think, and I wasn't going to get that at his place. "I think I'm going to head home."

"That anxious to get out of here, huh?" There was a lightness to his voice that let me know he understood.

"Not that I don't want to stay and hang out, but I'm ready for a shower."

"You didn't like the one in your room?"

"After having a strange guy nearly knock down your door, taking a shower was out of the question."

"You can take one now." He gestured to the guest room door.

"My clean clothes are at home anyway."

"Okay, either way. I'm not going to fight you on it considering you're not showering with me so I get no benefit from it."

I laughed. "You always do that."

"Do what?" He sipped his coffee, picking up a paper I hadn't even noticed him bring in.

"Throw in random sexual comments when I'm not expecting them."

"I don't know what you're talking about." His sheepish grin was kind of cute.

"You just implied you wanted to take a shower with me."

He shrugged. "Sometimes they just come out."

"Yeah, for me too. I did make the spoon comment."

He chuckled. "Yeah, but I took that one step further."

"I totally opened myself up for it."

"That you did." He set down the paper. "What did you think of Jared?"

Hot. I kept that thought to myself. "Pushy and arrogant."

"Yeah, doesn't surprise me. I'm sorry you had to deal with him."

"It wasn't a big deal." Hopefully, he'd never know about me wielding a lamp.

"Next time that happens, call me and don't open the door."

"Next time? That implies I'll be waking up here again."

"You will be. Preferably it won't be in my guest room though." He winked. "I guess I just did it again."

"You can be really weird." He was different from most of the guys I knew. He had confidence, but it came across almost geeky.

"Can I?"

"Yeah…but in a cute way."

"Does that mean you'll go out with me again?"

"Yes, but this time can I pick the restaurant?"

"Definitely…but I have a better idea."

"Oh yeah?" I asked with interest. Was he thinking about a place like that Sprite café again?

"Let's cook here. You spent more time checking out my kitchen than you do checking me out."

"That might be too tempting of an offer to turn down. When were you thinking?"

"Tomorrow night? I figure we can take one night off in between."

"All right. Is it safe to assume someone's going to be watching my apartment?" I knew I was in danger, but I wasn't going to let that get in the way of living my life. If having Toby set up security could help, I was okay with it.

"Yes. But they won't be watching you. I can assure you of that."

"I'd hope not…otherwise I might as well stay here."

"That offer's always on the table."

"I'll take my chances at home."

"All right. Let me finish this coffee and then I'll walk you home."

"You don't have to do that. I should be fine in broad daylight."

He smiled. "I don't have to, but I want to. Sometimes it's nice to get what you want."

***

"What are you staring at?" I caught Eric watching me for at least the third time Sunday afternoon. I wanted him to go back to his general policy of ignoring me unless he wanted to annoy me.

"I'm just looking in the same general direction of where you happen to be."

"Do you have to do that?"

"I don't have to, but I like to."

"Fantastic."

He got off his stool and strode toward me. I should have just ignored him. "Have a nice time with Toby?"

"It was fine." What was I supposed to say? He told me I'm in danger and you're either fantasizing about me in bed or worried that I'll be mauled by a wolf or bear. I shivered just thinking about either image. Not the good kind of shiver.

"I didn't even know you guys were friends."

"It turns out we have some mutual friends."

"You're into him." Eric's words weren't a question.

"Yeah."

He smiled slightly. "He's not who you think he is. Just remember that."

"Are you who I think you are?"

"No, but you're already afraid of me. You should have that feeling about Toby too."

"But I don't." I set aside the worn paperback of *Northanger Abbey* I was reading to kill the time. Late afternoons were quiet at work. We'd barely had any customers.

"That only makes him more dangerous."

"He's not going to hurt me." I felt that in every grain of my body. I knew he wasn't a saint, but he wasn't out to hurt me.

"Probably not. That's true."

"You admit that but still think I should be careful?"

"You should always be careful with the unknown, especially those that make you feel safe."

"Just tell me what the hell is going on. Who are you guys?" I crossed my legs, leaning forward slightly on my stool.

"Who do you think we are?"

"Honestly?"

"Yeah. Give me your best guess. If you get it right on the first try, I'll tell you."

I accepted the challenge. "Organized crime. Maybe not the Mafia but something like it."

"What gave you that idea?"

"The suits, mysterious hours, wild animals available to attack people."

"Wild animals available to attack? What kind of crime boss shows are you watching?"

"You told me you'd tell me if I was right."

"You're not right."

"Then who are you? None of this makes sense." I sighed.

"I can't tell you more about it. We're not together." He sat down on a stool and crossed his legs at his ankles.

"Excuse me?"

"You heard me. If you decided you wanted to be with me, I could fill you in."

"Be with you? As in date you?"

"More than date." His eyes moved up and down my body.

I crossed my arms to block his view. "Yeah…not happening."

"That was quick."

"You're not my type, Eric."

"But Toby is?"

"Maybe." I couldn't help but think about Jared. Physically he was my type, even if his personality wasn't.

"You're not my type either, but that doesn't stop me from liking you."

"I'm not your type?" I glared at him. "Then what? You're messing with me?" Not that I cared whether he liked me or not, but he was only confusing me more.

"I usually go for girls a little feistier than you."

"Feistier?" I sneered at him. "I'll show you feisty."

He laughed. "Glad to know you care so much."

"I don't care."

"Sure, sure. Get back to work, Bates." His teasing made me think that maybe he was going to back off.

Chapter Twelve

Toby

"Who the hell let you in here?" I snapped the second I walked through my office door. I'd reluctantly said goodbye to Casey at her apartment earlier, and I wasn't in the mood to deal with Jared yet.

He leaned back in my chair with his feet on my desk. "Hello, Toby. Nice to see you too. Your assistant let me in. A witch, isn't she? She's cute, although I think I like the girl you keep at home even better."

"Stay the hell away from Casey." I gave Jared a warning look. He was right about Nelly being a witch. She was the one who wiped my friends' minds and I owed her. If they hooked up, it wasn't my problem, but Casey wasn't up for discussion.

"Ah. Casey. I knew she had a name. And I seem to have hit a nerve. Funny, she seemed to think you two were just friends." He grinned wickedly, knowing just how to get me where it hurt.

"She's unavailable."

"Is she? I wouldn't go after another Pteron's mate—unlike some other people." He put his hands behind his head.

"Allie was mine first."

"She wasn't your mate. But that's beside the point. We're talking about Casey, and she isn't your mate either."

I growled. "Just leave her alone."

"Okay. I get it. You like the girl."

"Is there a real reason you're here, or is it just to annoy me?"

"I'm here because you suck at your job."

"My men are on it."

"That's not good enough and you know it. We have to quash this before it gets any bigger." He leaned back further in my chair, and I had to fight myself not to toss him from it. It wasn't worth the fall out.

"What do you suggest we do?" I stayed standing. I refused to sit in one of my visitor chairs. He'd like that too much.

"Who do you have on the inside?"

"I've got a guy." Marv wasn't ideal, but it would have to do.

"Wolf? Bear?" He sounded bored.

"Bear. We're watching him closely."

"Have you mapped out the attacks yet? Do they fit any pattern?" He messed with the pens on my desk.

I shook my head. "No. They just keep getting progressively more public."

"I want to avoid any outright fighting. That will just give them the attention they're looking for. We have to do this quietly. I'll need to look at everything you have on the packs and clans involved."

"I'll get their files." My grandfather had been so old school that we literally had file folders. I planned on changing everything over to an electronic system when I got the chance.

"Good. Anything fun going on tonight?" He cracked a smile, and I knew he was messing with me.

"No." I planned to comb through all the documents myself. Like hell I was going to let him discover anything first. Jared may have been Levi's best, but he distracted easily. I needed to prove I could handle the situation myself if I didn't want more of Laurent's men on my territory.

"Are you positive?"

"I'm sure you can find something to do."

"Maybe I should see if Casey's free…"

"She's not." I regretted my decision to hold off on our dinner date until the next night.

"Are you sure? She seemed to really like me this morning." He was just pushing my buttons, but it pissed me off.

"Try the witches' place in Battery Park." Anything to keep him away from Casey. I'm sure he'd find something or someone to keep him busy there.

"Maybe I will."

"Great, now get out of my office." I pointed to the open door.

"I thought we were just starting to have some fun."

"Go bother someone else."

"Will do, but get me those files. I'll need an office for the time I'm here."

"You're not going to be here long."

He finally got his damn feet off my desk. "I still need an office."

"Fine. Ask Nelly."

"Sounds like a plan." He got out of my chair. "Try to calm down. Stress isn't good for you."

"Fuck you," I grumbled. Even if he weren't a cocky bastard, I'd still hate him. He reminded me of everything I hated about Levi—only worse. He'd better stay far away from Casey. She already had Eric to worry about, she didn't need Jared too. She didn't need me either, but it was probably too late for that. She'd awakened a side in me I thought was gone, and I needed it. I dug out my phone as Jared strolled out through the doorway.

"Hey, Toby," Casey answered in a singsong tone. She sounded happy to hear from me.

"Hey. Any chance we can move that dinner date up to tonight?"

"Miss me already?" she teased.

"Yes." No reason to beat around the bush. Maybe part of my motivation was another Pteron, but I still wanted to see her.

"Honesty. I like that."

I glanced at my watch. "Are you still at work?"

"No. I'm home, but didn't you know that?"

"How would I know that?"

"You have me under surveillance." She didn't sound as annoyed about it as I would have thought. We'd only been hanging out for a few days, but I already knew to expect the unexpected with her. Her reactions were hard to predict, and there was something exciting about it. My work life had been stressful, but my personal life had been as boring as they come. The change was good.

"I don't ask for minute to minute updates. I just want to know if there's anything suspicious."

"Ah, I see. I'll run to the store and meet you at your place." She sounded excited, and I wanted to see her.

"Do you really need to do the shopping yourself? We could have someone else do it." That would give us more time to hang out at home. God, I sounded like an old person. Dinner at home was okay for one night, but I'd have to take her out somewhere nice next time.

"Seriously? Seriously, Toby?" Her voice rose a little, and I could just picture her incredulous expression.

"What? I'm just saying…"

"We're going to the market like normal people."

"We? So I'm invited?"

"Oh. I guess I did say that." She sounded surprised about her words. "Yeah. You're invited if you want."

"I'm leaving my office now. Wait for me."

"I will."

I'd never been more excited for food shopping in my life.

Chapter Thirteen

Jared

Toby was too easy to rile up. Usually it took me a while to find someone's weak spots, the things they were most sensitive about, but not this time. Maybe I was getting better which, beyond being fun, was part of my job. I needed to find ways to get people to think and feel what I wanted them to. Strictly speaking, I didn't need to mess with Toby, but it was too simple to resist.

There was something about that girl, Casey, that he wanted. She was attractive. There was no question about that. Even in the oversized clothes I could tell she had a great body, and that pretty face of hers wasn't anything to brush off either. Still, it had to be more than that. There were lots of pretty girls out there, and Toby seemed bent out of shape over this one. But they weren't a couple. She'd made that part crystal clear. Was she doing that for my benefit? I wasn't going to seek her out, but if she came to me, I wouldn't hold back on his account.

I pushed Casey from my mind and focused on my plans for the night. Glad I'd thrown a blazer in with my clothes, I got ready to go out. I'd never been out in New York without Levi and Owen, but I didn't let that stop me. There was no way I was sitting around and staring at the walls all night. Besides, it might actually help me figure out what the hell was going on.

I hadn't taken a trip up to the city in a while, so I decided to take Toby's suggestion and check out the place in Battery Park. A paranormal club would serve my purposes for the evening. The paranormal bars in New Orleans are what you'd expect them to be. Picture biker bars with stronger liquor and more dangerous clientele. I already knew this place would be different. Any place run by witches was bound to be trouble.

I decided to fly over, so I carried the rest of my clothes with me. There was something cool about flying in New York City at night. As much as I'm a New Orleans guy, nothing beats that skyline, and it looks even better from above. I had to fly high up to avoid being spotted, but I stayed close enough to enjoy the view. I landed in the park and quickly got changed. Shirt buttoned and blazer on, I headed inside.

"Florence, what the hell are you doing here?" The bouncer recognized me immediately when I stepped up to the entrance. He looked like a Silver Back. Those gorilla shifters were built large.

"Glad to see me?" I had no clue who the guy was.

"No. I'm never glad to see you."

"Really? Is there a particular reason why not?" I could have pushed him out of the way, but his annoyance was actually kind of amusing.

"Yeah, you slept with my sister."

"I doubt that." I made it my business to stay away from anyone not human. "I don't do shifter trash."

"She's adopted, jackass. "

"Oh. Well, did she complain?"

He lunged for me, and I easily caught his fist. "Let's not make a scene. We both know who'd win a fight."

He grunted but stepped out of my way so I could enter.

I pushed my way through the crowds looking for the bar. Work or not, I wasn't spending a night with a bunch of tight ass paranormals sober.

A pretty redhead winked at me. I ignored her. She was a witch, and I didn't want to mess with magic.

"What can I get you?" the bartender asked. I couldn't tell exactly what he was, but I had a feeling he was shifter.

"A Jack and Coke."

"Coming up." He made the drink and set it down in front of me. "Are you new in town?"

"I'm only here for a visit."

"Oh yeah? Where you from?"

"New Orleans." I took a large swig of the drink.

"What do you think of the new king? Is he going to make it?"

"Of course, he is. He's exactly what The Society needs." I was fiercely defensive of Levi. He was the one guy I knew who would always have my back, and I always had his.

The bartender looked at me warily, probably realizing I was a Pteron and he was treading on thin ice.

"Jared, hello." A cute, blonde witch put a hand on my arm. "So nice of you to stop by The Sprite House."

"I thought I'd make the rounds."

"Lovely. Let me show you around." She linked her arm with mine.

"You're the second high-ranking Pteron we've had in here in the last few weeks."

"Oh yeah?" I feigned interest, already staking out the place for intel. I wasn't going to get it from a witch.

"Toby. Our new fearless leader."

"Oh, really? I didn't think he ever left his office." Just because he dropped the name didn't mean he frequented the place.

"He did. Had a pretty little human with him too."

Now that got my interest. "A brunette, big blue eyes?"

"Uh huh. You know her?"

"In passing."

"He got bent out of shape when I enchanted her drink with an aphrodisiac spell. I've never seen a man push a girl away more. He's too noble for his own good."

"Tsk tsk. Enchanting a Pteron's date is a no-no."

"Not by our rules. I didn't enchant him."

"I'm surprised he didn't shut you down." I was also surprised he'd kept her at arm's length. I doubted I'd have that kind of restraint with her. If she asked for it, she'd get it from me.

"He was all right with it once I explained that all it did was enhance feelings." The witch let her hand move up my arm until she squeezed my bicep. "It was an ego boost."

"Was that true? The enhance part?"

"Yeah. The more the girl already feels, the better it works."

"Good for him." I wondered if he was being as noble at that moment. My guess was he had her in his bed already. Damn, I needed to stop thinking about the girl. I had to focus on the job and not the growing bulge in my pants.

The witch noticed it too. The way her eyes zeroed in on my crotch left me wondering if witches had better vision than I thought. Maybe she just had a sense for hard-ons. "Is that for me, or are you thinking about Toby's girl?"

"She's not his."

"What is it with you Pterons always fighting over the same humans? Didn't Levi and Toby just go to war last year?" With a sly grin, she released my arm and wandered off.

"A Pteron, huh?"

I followed the seductive voice and found a girl with jet black hair down to her waist. She sat in a darkened booth in a circular alcove. She had a friend with her with equally long hair that was blonde.

"Maybe. What's it to you?"

"What kind are you?" The blonde stood up and gestured for me to slip into the booth between them. If I was at a human bar, I would have been all about it, but these weren't humans.

I shook my head. "I'm fine where I am."

"Are you sure?" she reached behind her neck, untying the strings of her halter top.

"Absolutely." I kept myself in check. She wasn't human, which meant she wasn't of interest in that department.

"That's too bad. We thought you wanted to have some fun with us." She dropped the strings and exposed her bare chest.

I swallowed. Human men would pay big money for a few minutes in a place like that.

"You heard him. He's not interested." The dark haired girl spoke, and by the time I turned to look at her, she was also topless.

"But he's straight. I can tell," the blonde whined. She stepped toward me as though she wasn't half naked.

"Maybe he's the type that likes to watch."

Fuck. They were nymphs. Only nymphs would be playing with me like that. I turned around to regain my composure for a second. By the time I turned back, the blonde was crawling onto her friend's lap.

"What I want from you is information."

"Information?" The blonde turned around and slid into the seat next to her friend. Neither bothered to cover up even though the subject had changed.

"Yes."

"What will we get?"

"That depends on how good the information is."

"How good does it have to be to get a fuck out of you?" the blonde asked without missing a beat.

"That's not happening. I could compensate you in other ways."

She pouted. "Money can buy us things."

The dark haired nymph giggled. "Fun things."

I probably could have found someone else to question, but drunk nymphs are easy to interrogate, and human or not, neither had a bad rack. After all, there is a saying about being able to look but not touch. Nymphs talked, they also listened and did a lot of fucking. My guess is these girls had been in bed with plenty of bears and wolves lately and probably had lots to tell.

"You could at least sit down."

"I suppose I could." I walked back out to the bar and picked up a chair. Sliding into that booth wouldn't be a good idea.

"You really are no fun."

"My clothes are staying on, ladies."

"Even your shirt?" The blonde touched her breasts, as though accentuating her nakedness would make me want to do the same thing. "You could at least show us your wings."

"Good to know that if the money dries up, I can sell nudie shots to the nymphs."

They both giggled. "You could sell more than a picture."

"Okay. Let's stay on task here." I pulled out a fifty from my wallet and placed it on the table. The girls turned their eyes to the paper. "All right, good. The attacks, tell me about them."

"What do you want to know?" The blonde picked up the bill and tucked it into her skirt so that half of it stuck out. I wasn't asking for it back even if they didn't talk.

"Why now? Who's the ring leader?"

"The king is weak."

"No, he's not." I could feel my anger boil. They might be seeing my wings for a whole different reason.

"He is, and there're some secrets the bears have uncovered."

"Secrets?"

"Yes. Big secrets."

I pulled out another fifty. This time, the dark haired girl took it. "They're trying to get the king to strike back, to give them an excuse to make a real run against them."

"But they struck first."

"Only on humans…not on the Pterons." She lay down, resting her head on her friend's lap.

"What kind of timeline are we talking?"

"Fast." The blonde squeezed her friend's breast, making the other girl moan. It was time to leave before things got out of hand.

"I'll send some willing participants your way."

"Are you sure you don't want to join us? I promise you'll have a good time." The brunette sat up, placed the cash on the table, and started sliding her skirt down over her tan hips. She wasn't wearing any panties.

"Yeah, I bet. Later, ladies." I resisted the urge to glance back but tapped the first guy I saw on the shoulder. "Do you do nymphs?"

"Who doesn't?"

"Me. But there're two naked ones back there looking for some company."

"Really?"

"Yeah."

The guy looked at me like I was Santa Claus.

I shook my head and walked right out. I didn't even have a second sip of my drink. I picked up my phone and called Owen. New York was even crazier than I remembered.

Chapter Fourteen

Casey

"I didn't expect to be back here so soon." I set two brown grocery bags down on the island in Toby's kitchen.

"We already had plans for tomorrow night, so it shouldn't be that surprising." He set down his bags and started unpacking.

"Yeah, but I barely even left." I glanced around at the spick and span kitchen. I wondered if Toby cleaned it himself, or if he hired someone to do it. Probably the latter.

"You say it like it's a bad thing."

"Not necessarily bad, just surprising."

"Have you had many boyfriends?" He watched me closely, as though he was afraid of missing my reaction.

"I've had my share." That was a bit of an exaggeration, but I wasn't going to admit how little I'd dated.

"Serious ones?"

"Not really." There was only one guy who'd gotten under my skin. He'd also been the only one to break my heart.

"Hmm."

"Why are you asking?" I crossed my arms. I didn't enjoy the interrogation. My love life was definitely not an approved topic of conversation.

"I'm just curious." There was something about his expression that made me doubt him. He didn't seem to be asking out of a competitive need to know either. I wanted to know more about his answer, but I couldn't dig for more information unless I was ready to give up some secrets of my own.

"All right, ready to start cooking?"

He nodded. "Sure."

I dug out the flour and cut up the butter for the roux. Toby was getting a lesson in making sauces.

"Who taught you how to cook?" Toby easily followed my directions as I had him prepare and bread the chicken breasts.

"My mom. It's kind of our thing." I missed cooking with her. It was one of the few things I missed about being home. I'd had a nice enough childhood, but I always felt kind of out of sorts, like I didn't quite fit in. That's probably why I jumped at the chance to date the first bad boy I could. He was everything my parents had warned me about, but that just made it better. If I'd known the trouble it would cause, I would have walked the other way when he first smiled at me.

Toby pulled me out of my thoughts. "That's cool. I grew up with my dad mostly. His cooking usually involved take-out."

"It's great that you're making an effort to teach yourself."

He shrugged awkwardly, and I realized he was trying to scratch an itch without getting any of the egg and breadcrumb mixture on his face.

"Let me help you with that." I reached up and scratched where I thought he needed it.

"Thanks." He smiled.

My face was still close to his from when I'd leaned in. "You're welcome."

His lips crushed into mine without warning, and I eagerly responded.

"Don't move." He quickly washed his hands before picking me up and placing me on one of the few clean spots on the counter.

His lips returned to mine, and we effortlessly got back to where we'd been. I wrapped my arms around his neck, and his hands rested on my legs. His tongue pushed into my mouth and tangled with mine in every possible way.

I leaned back, hitting my head on the upper cabinet. "Ow."

"You okay?" He touched my head where I'd hit it.

"Absolutely." I pulled his face back to mine. Then someone knocked on the door. I groaned as Toby stepped back and walked out of the kitchen.

"Whoever it is, this better be important." His words carried across the apartment.

"It's me," a male voice answered.

I smoothed out my hair, trying to hide signs of what we'd been doing as Toby answered the door.

"Make this fast."

I hopped off the counter and put the chicken in the oven before peeking around the corner to watch Toby talk to a guy I hadn't seen before. At least it wasn't Jared. I didn't need to see him after making out with Toby.

They were talking in hushed tones, so I decided to take a look out the window and wait them out. They talked for a few more minutes before I heard Toby close the door.

"You have such an amazing view." I stood with my eyes glued out the living room windows. I loved the city, and would never get tired of watching the constant bustle of it all. I decided not to ask about the visitor. I was positive he'd just give me an evasive answer, like everything else.

"That's why I picked this place."

"Do you own or rent?"

"Own."

"Why am I not surprised?"

He laughed. "It's an investment."

"How long have you lived here? Just since January?" He mentioned that he'd finished one semester at Princeton, and I assumed he hadn't commuted that far.

"I moved in right after the holidays."

"Cool. If you're ever looking for a roommate, look no further." Had I really just said that out loud?

He grinned. "This from the girl so adamantly opposed to spending the night? If you move in here, it won't be as my roommate."

"It won't?" I liked the teasing. There was something hot about it, and it made me want him more.

"How blatant do I have to make things? Did what happened in the kitchen not make it clear?"

I licked my lips. "It helped."

"Does that mean you wouldn't be surprised if I tried to kiss you again right now?" There was a twinkle in his eyes that made him seem younger, less serious than usual.

"Not surprised, but—"

My response was cut off when his lips brushed against mine softly. "What were you going to say?" He cradled my head in his hands and watching me intently.

"Nothing important."

"Good." He moved his lips against mine again, slow at first and then faster. I didn't expect it to become anything more when he nipped my lip softly and slipped his tongue into my mouth. I gladly let him deepen the kiss, reaching up to wrap my arms around his neck again. One of his hands slipped down to my back where he used it to pull me against him. I could have kissed him for hours, loving the frenzied way his mouth moved against mine and the way he tasted like a cross between mint and something earthy. I wanted more, but eventually he broke the kiss.

"I had no idea kissing you would be this good." I rested my head against his chest.

"Yeah? It's how I've been picturing it."

I picked up my head so I could look at him. "You've been picturing it?"

"For a while now." He half shrugged in a way that made him seem almost embarrassed. A guy that could kiss like that should never feel embarrassed.

"I've pictured it too." I also pictured doing a whole lot more with him, but kissing repeatedly was a really good start.

"Good to know."

The incessant beeping from the kitchen let us know the chicken was ready.

"I guess we need to check on the food."

"Yeah, I guess so." He walked toward the kitchen. "Maybe we can try out some more of that kissing later."

"Maybe..." The maybe was a yes.

Chapter Fifteen

Toby

Casey was asleep in my guest room again. I'd have much preferred her in my bed, but that would have pushed things way too fast. She'd been the one to suggest staying over this time. She claimed it was the much more comfortable bed, but I sensed she also liked being at my place. I hoped I was right.

I got the feeling she was far more innocent than she pretended to be, but asking her more about it was out of the question. Until I found out for certain whether she was a virgin, I sure as hell wasn't pushing her to do anything too fast, even if it meant waking up with such a hard-on nothing was going to fix it. Well, nothing but her.

I was fully prepared to take care of the situation myself when I heard her tentative knock.

"Come in." I responded automatically, even if I was lying in bed in just a pair of boxers.

She pushed open the door and hesitated in the doorway. "Oh, did I wake you up?"

Not in the way she thought she did. "No, I've been up. Do you need anything?"

"I have to be at work in an hour, so I wanted to tell you I'm heading out."

"If you can wait a second, I'll walk you." I got out of bed, throwing back the covers without thinking about what she was going to see.

Her eyes widened and she blushed. "I can walk myself."

I quickly slipped into some gym shorts. "It's really not a problem."

She kept staring at the ground. "Okay. I'll meet you at the front door."

By her embarrassed response, I was pretty sure my original theory was right. Casey was a virgin, and I was just going to have to sit back and wait for her to be ready.

I finished getting dressed and met Casey. "Ready?"

"Yup." She seemed pretty eager to leave, and I hoped it was because she wanted time to get ready rather than wanting to get out of my apartment.

We walked back to her cousin's place quietly. I started to open my mouth a few times, but realized I had no idea what to say. All too quickly, we were standing outside her building.

I turned to look at her. "Are you working late tonight?"

"Yeah. I'm covering Remy's shift. I close."

"Oh, okay. If you want to hang out afterward let me know."

"It's going to be pretty late." She pulled her keys out of her purse.

I smiled at her. I only needed to sleep an hour or two at night. "I don't mind staying up."

She bit her lip, and it made me want to kiss her again. "I'll give you a call when I'm out."

Nice. Maybe I could get used to the whole dating thing again. "Sounds good. Have a great day."

"You too." She leaned up like she was going to kiss me but then stopped and started unlocking the door.

"Casey?"

She turned, and I placed a feather light kiss on her lips. "See you tonight."

She smiled. "See you tonight."

I waited until she made it inside before heading back home to get changed for the day. Casey wasn't the only one who needed to work.

***

"There're two of you now?" I groaned, annoyed to see that in addition to Jared sitting behind my desk, Owen, Levi's advisor, was also camped out in my office.

"Hey, man." Owen nodded at me like we actually knew each other.

"Did Levi send you too?" How little did the king trust me that he had to send up two of his men to babysit?

"No. I'm just keeping Jared company." He smirked at Jared who responded by tossing my globe at Owen's head. Lucky for them, Owen caught it before it broke. That globe was one of the few things of my mom's that I'd bothered to keep. I would have been beyond pissed if they smashed it.

"Jared needs someone to keep him company?"

"It's boring up here." Jared tried to shrug it off, but I could tell he was embarrassed at the insinuation that he couldn't handle something on his own. I understood the feeling.

That didn't mean I was going to let him get away with putting his dirty shoes on my desk again. "Get out of my chair."

"You didn't care yesterday."

"That's because I thought it was a one-time visit. It's not happening today."

"Ah, I get it."

"You do? Then why aren't you moving?"

"You didn't get laid, did you? Casey freezing you out? I've seen what that can do to a guy." He grinned.

I did to, but I wasn't admitting he was right. "Get out of my chair."

"Fine, chill out." He got up and took a seat on the window sill.

"I'm hoping you have news." If they were just there to annoy me, they'd have it coming to them.

"I did some digging last night while you were busy not screwing your girl."

"Just spit it out."

"There's something major going down. I don't have details, but I can tell they're planning something big."

"Something big? Is that all you have?"

Jared slid off the window and started to pace. "I need to talk to your inside man."

"I'll talk to him for you."

"No." He scowled. "I'll do it myself."

"He knows me. He'll tell me more."

"And I work directly for the king. I hold more authority, and he'll respond to that."

"No one up here gives a damn about the king." Myself included, but I didn't say that part out loud.

"Is that what you think? Those little chicken shits can't even look me in the eye, they're so scared of him."

"They can't look you in the eye because they hate you and the king."

Owen laughed. "Harsh."

"But true."

Jared stopped right in front of me. "Why would they hate the king? He's not the one who killed their leader."

I glared at him. "Shut the fuck up, Florence. This has nothing to do with my grandfather. It has to do with New Orleans acting like they're better than us. New Yorkers don't take well to being told a decaying southern city holds more sway."

"Decaying southern city?" Jared got up in my face. "Is that what you think?"

I didn't blink. "It's a trash heap. We all know it."

Jared's eyes started turning black and Owen grabbed him. "He's just messing with you, man. Let it go."

"No. No fucking way this asshat with a stick up his ass is going to put down NOLA."

"I'm an asshat and I have a stick up my ass? Very original."

"Drop it, Toby." Owen said it quietly, but there was a warning in his words. I knew I could probably hold my own in a fight with Jared, but we had bigger problems to deal with.

"If I call in my guy, will you guys get out of here?"

"Why are you in such a hurry to get rid of us? Are you hiding something?" Jared's eyes were slowly fading back to their usual brown.

"No, I just want some peace and quiet."

"Come on, Toby. You know you love having us around." Jared had an annoying way of glazing over things and falling back on sarcasm.

"I'll make the call." I picked up the phone and called Tim. This was one of those things that would look bad if I did it myself. "Get Marv in here now."

"Is there a reason why?"

"The reason is that two crows are sitting in my office."

Jared chuckled. "I heard that, hawk boy."

Pterons are tied to a variety of birds, and although we view each other as superior to all other shifters, we don't particularly like each other.

"I'll get him." Tim hung up.

My cousin could be annoying, but he got the job done. They'd been more than happy to step up and work for me when my grandfather died, and they'd proven themselves more useful than I originally anticipated.

I wanted to grill Tim about any updates on Casey's place, but I wasn't doing that in front of Jared. With any luck, Eric would accompany his uncle in and I'd learn more. I cared too much about her to just sit back and wait. I wanted to hit whoever was after her head on. I was going to find out who was after Casey and why, but I hated the sinking feeling that she was hiding something from me. She got weird when I'd asked about past boyfriends, and my gut told me it all tied in. As long as she hadn't dated other Pterons, I'd be okay. I wasn't ready to deal with that again.

"How long's it going to take?" Jared asked.

"Not long."

"Where can I get a cup of coffee around here?"

"There's a Starbucks downstairs."

"No complimentary coffee for your guests?"

"You're not my guests, but there's some down the hall."

"Thanks. We'll be back." They walked out of the room.

I settled into my desk chair and treated myself to a few more thoughts of Casey. It had been ages since I'd craved a girl, and as sexually frustrated as I felt, I preferred the feeling to the numbness that had been there before. I sent her a text. *You didn't make me coffee this morning.*

After sending it, I realized she might not check her phone at work. She answered that question when she replied a minute later. *I'll make you some tonight.*

I smiled. Even better.

Chapter Sixteen

Casey

No matter how many times I did it, I hated closing. I didn't do it alone. Eric always seemed to be with me, but there was something about having to stay around long after everyone else left that I didn't like. It was also right before closing that the biggest weirdos came in. Sometimes they were there to see Eric, but other times they just seemed to want coffee and nearly stale pastries.

I was busy mentally recounting my kiss with Toby for the hundredth time when the bell dinged signaling someone entering the store. Eric was out back dumping the trash. He'd taken Rhett to heart and didn't make me do it anymore. "Can I help you?"

Thanks to a pair of tinted glasses and a hood, I had no idea who the person in front of me was, but my skin crawled as the figure stepped closer. The figure was large, so I assumed it was a male, but I had no clue.

"Casey Bates," the mystery figure asked in a deep voice. Definitely male.

My chest tightened. How did he know my name?

"Are you Casey?" he asked again.

"Maybe." I took a deep breath. Eric would be back in soon.

He chuckled. I wouldn't have expected someone like that to even know how to laugh. "I'll take that as a yes. Not that I didn't know already."

"What do you want with her?" I grabbed hold of the counter. My heart was beating a million miles a minute.

"Nothing sinister, I assure you."

Where was Eric? Surely dumping trash couldn't take that long. That is unless there was a wolf out there again. "Do you want to order something?"

He laughed again. "It says a lot about your strength that you're still the polite barista."

"Sir, if you're not going to order something, I need to ask you to leave." I tried to still my shaking body. Something about this guy gave me the creeps. The fact that I couldn't see his eyes made it so much worse.

"Ask me to leave?"

"Yes. If you read that sign, we have the right to refuse service."

"Maybe it's time we both stop playing games, Casey."

"Who are you?" A strange sense of familiarity hit me.

"She misses you."

Those were the only words I needed to hear. "Where is she? What did you do to her?"

"Calm down, Casey. Vera is doing just fine."

"Can I see her?" Those three words may have been the most stupid I'd ever uttered, but I missed my sister more than anything. I didn't know what kind of trouble she was in, but I knew I'd never stop trying to find her. This was the closest I'd ever come.

"Yes." He didn't hesitate with his answer, and that terrified me.

"When?"

"Now. I'll take you to her."

"Why?" I still remembered the day Vera disappeared like it was yesterday and not years ago. After a two month investigation, the police closed the file. They said she probably ran off with her boyfriend, but I knew better. She would never leave without saying goodbye to me. I knew in my heart she was still alive out there somewhere.

"Because she wants to see you." He stepped closer to the counter.

"Why now?" I knew the timing couldn't be a coincidence. Why wait so long?

"Two reasons."

"Which are?"

"You've grown up, and you're in danger."

"I'm in danger? Why do people keep telling me that?"

"Because it's true." He rested his gloved hands right in front of me.

"Who am I in danger from?"

"I'll tell you if you come with me." His voice was slightly scratchy and it made him sound even more frightening.

I felt like I was in one of those after school specials. The ones where they dramatize an abduction, and you watch, telling yourself you'd never be stupid enough to fall for the trick. "Can't you just tell me what I need to know?"

I heard a crash and Eric limped into the room. "Run, Bates!"

"What? Are you okay?" I gaped at him, he was covered in blood.

"Run!"

Instinct kicked in, and I listened. I headed to the door, but the faceless guy blocked me. "No need to run, Casey. We can walk." He grabbed my arm.

"Let go of me."

"Not going to happen." He gripped my arm tighter.

"Run," Eric hissed. I turned around in time to watch Eric punch the guy. The man stumbled back, releasing my arm in the process.

"Run!" Eric didn't need to say it again.

I hit the pavement and didn't look back. My initial thought was to go home, but that was the first place anyone would look for me. I didn't want to lead anyone to Remy either. I once again went with instinct and headed to Toby's building.

The doorman opened the door, recognizing me. "Are you here to see Mr. Welsh?"

"Yes." I tried to calm my breathing.

"I'm afraid he's not in right now. He's been out all day."

I glanced outside, praying no one had followed me.

"Are you in some trouble, Miss?"

I nodded. "I need to see him."

His demeanor suddenly changed, he straightened and looked me right in the eye. "Who's after you?"

"I don't know."

He pulled out his phone and called someone. "I need back up. The girl's here and she's being followed. That's fine, send someone."

He pocketed his phone. "You're safe."

I nodded, hoping he was right.

His words were proved wrong moments later when the glass in the front door shattered into pieces and scattered on the floor in front of us.

"Get down!" the doorman yelled, stepping in front of me.

"She's with us," the creepy guy from Coffee Heaven spat. He strode into the lobby, walking right over the glass shards. He wasn't wearing his hood or glasses anymore, and I wanted to vomit. Deep inside, I knew it was him, but seeing his face just proved he did know where my sister was. Standing in front of me was her boyfriend, Murphy, the one she met because I dated his younger brother. I still hadn't forgiven myself for introducing them.

"She's not with you." Toby stormed into the lobby, only it didn't really look like Toby. His eyes were completely black, and he had large brown wings extending out of his shirtless back. I knew with complete certainty this wasn't his first time saving me. I also knew he wasn't human, and that was almost as scary as my sister's ex-boyfriend.

"Taking up with Pterons already?" Murphy seethed.

"Pterons?" I said the strange term slowly, surprised I even had the capacity to speak. I heard shouting from outside, and I wondered if it was the police.

"She's with me. Get the fuck out of here." Toby strode over to Murphy with the most menacing expression I'd ever seen.

Murphy sneered. "What do you want with her? She's of no use to you."

"But she's of use to you?" Toby asked in a strained voice. It was like he was struggling to hold on.

"Lots of use. So if you don't mind, I'll be taking what's mine."

"Like hell you are." Toby's fist made contact with Murphy's face and he flew into the pile of glass by the door. The temperature seemed to rise and there was a slight haziness. When I blinked my eyes, instead of Murphy, I saw a large grizzly bear.

I stepped back as far as I could until my back made contact with the wall.

"Get her out of here, Cody!" Toby tossed the doorman a set of keys.

"To the estate?"

"Yes."

I barely registered what was happening when Cody grabbed my arm and pulled me out of the lobby.

"Let go of me!" I fought against his arms, but it did nothing.

"Calm down. I'm not going to hurt you."

Like I was going to believe a word he said. He was listening to a man with wings, and he didn't even bat an eye when another man turned into a bear.

"I don't want to restrain you, but I will if that's what it takes to get your cooperation." He towed me toward a silver Acura SUV. Over my shoulder, I watched Toby lunge at a bear that had been a man moments earlier.

Restrain me? I did the sane thing and started to scream.

The screaming didn't last long. A hand clamped down over my mouth and within seconds, I was on the floor of the backseat with my arms tied. How had he moved so fast? And why was no one noticing the manhandling?

Damn it. He tied my legs, and put tape over my mouth before slamming the door and going around to the front.

I tried to scream, but nothing came out around the tape.

"I know it doesn't seem that way, but you're with the good guys." Cody pulled out onto the street. "I don't know what those bears wanted with you, but it can't be good. Risking an open attack on a Pteron isn't something shifters like that do."

Shifters? Is that what that bear was? Like a wearwolf, but a bear? And there was that Pteron word again.

"Toby wants you out of harm's way, so I'll take you somewhere safe. You can thank me later."

Thank him? More like kick him in the balls.

I continued struggling, unwilling to go down without a fight. A few minutes later, Cody's cell phone rang. "She's fine. Maybe uncomfortable, but fine." He turned to look at me. "I had no choice. She screamed. She would have brought more danger upon herself. I'll make sure she knows that. See you then."

"Toby says he's sorry it had to come to this. He wishes he could have protected you better."

I struggled to talk again.

"If I take off that tape, will you be good?"

I nodded. I'd agree to anything to get that tape off.

He reached back and pulled off the tape in one quick motion. It hurt, but the relief was instant. I took in a large breath before speaking. "Who the hell are you people?"

"I'm not sure where to start."

"Start at the beginning."

"Has Toby told you anything?" He sped up.

"Just that I was in danger and he was dangerous."

"You didn't notice anything different about him?"

"I thought he was a crime boss." That was the only thing I'd come up with. I knew he was into something weird, but I thought mafia, not wings.

"I'm really not supposed to talk about this stuff with a human, but I guess the cat is out of the bag now. Nothing I say is going to be worse than what you saw." He paused before continuing. "Toby's a ranking Pteron. He runs New York for the king."

I laughed. "The king?"

"Yes. The King of The Society."

"What's a Pteron?"

"You saw his wings."

"So he's a fallen angel or something?"

Cody laughed. "We're not angels."

"We? You have wings too?"

"Yes." He tossed some weird plastic mask on the chair next to him. He turned around, and I gasped. It was a completely different person looking back at me. Young and with a shock of red hair, Cody didn't resemble the quiet, middle aged doorman I'd seen over the past few days.

"If you're not angels, then what are you?"

"We're bird shifters. Toby and I are tied to hawks."

"Yeah…right."

"I'm telling you the truth."

"And the bears?"

"What about them?" He continued driving quickly. The late hour left the streets mostly empty.

"Who are they?"

"Their official name is Urusus, but we don't call them that. The name sounds too distinguished for them. You can ask your boss about it though."

"My boss? You mean Marv?"

He made a sharp turn, and my head smashed into the seat in front of me. "Ouch."

He slowed down and then the car stopped. I tensed as I waited for the door to open.

"Marv and his nephew." He picked up the conversation like we hadn't stopped it. He scooped me off the floor and buckled me into a seat. "Sorry about that. Toby's going to kill me when he sees your head."

I could feel the blood before it flowed down my face enough to see it. Cody took a cloth out of his pocket and dabbed my forehead. "We'll be there in a few hours. You might as well try to rest. I have a feeling it's going to be a crazy night."

He closed my door and immediately locked it once he was back in the driver's seat. Even though I was still tied up, I could at least look out the window.

"Any other questions?"

"What does Toby want from me?" We were on some sort of interstate. From what I could tell, we were heading west of the city.

"Want from you?" Cody caught my eye in the rearview mirror. "Isn't that obvious?"

"Should it be?"

"He likes you. He hasn't shown this kind of interest since I started working with him."

"So he doesn't want to kill me?"

Cody laughed. "Kill you? Is that what you think every guy trying to get in your pants wants to do?"

"Most guys don't have wings and tell their friends to kidnap me."

"If you think this is bad, I can assure you being with the bears would be worse. I don't know what that guy wanted with you, but it couldn't be good."

"Where are you taking me?"

"To the Blackwell country estate."

"The Blackwell estate?"

"It's Toby's family name. He's running it now."

A question nudged at the corner of my mind, even though there were probably tons of more important ones to ask. "What happened to Toby's grandfather?"

Cody didn't say anything for a second. "I'll let him tell you."

"Why? All he told me was that he died."

"Yeah. It's Toby's story to tell."

"Then it can't be good."

"It's not." Cody turned on the radio, probably trying to signal to me that the conversation was over.

I used the break from conversation to formulate a plan. I had no idea what messed up stuff I was dealing with, but my sister was apparently part of it. Maybe if I played my cards right, I could get to her. My gut told me Toby had been telling me the truth when he said he wasn't dangerous to me, but that didn't mean I was going to listen to him blindly. I'd stay alert and find a way to get to Vera. Whatever the Blackwell estate was, I hoped it wasn't some crazy prison with a torture chamber. I'd play along if I needed to. Maybe those acting classes in high school would pay off.

Cody's phone rang again. He turned off the radio. "Hello. I'll ask her." He turned back toward me. "Are you hungry?"

"Are you really asking me that?"

"Toby said to make sure you ate something."

I laughed. It was the uncontrollable "I'm in over my head" kind of laugh.

"Hold on. Talk to her yourself." He must have hit the speaker button because Toby's voice came through the receiver. "You okay, Casey?"

"Never better."

"Sarcasm. That's a good sign." His voice was tense, but I could tell he was trying hard to put me at ease. Considering my hands were tied behind me, and I had no clue what I was in for, nothing was going to put me at ease.

"What the hell is going on?"

"I don't know. All hell has broken loose here. I'll get to you as soon as I can."

I needed answers. "What are you?"

"I can't talk much now, but I promise to tell you everything later."

The brush off wasn't going to fly. "You're a bird shifter?"

"Well, our shifter form is a hybrid. I don't turn into an actual hawk."

"You just sprout giant wings."

"Pretty much."

"Any other skills I should know about?"

"Strength, speed, agility, sexual prowess."

"Toby!"

He laughed. "I had to lighten things up. I'll be there as soon as I can, and I'm sorry. I should have protected you."

"Toby."

"Yeah?"

"You're not going to kill me?"

"Of course not!"

"I'm holding you to it!" I must have been losing my mind.

Chapter Seventeen

Toby

There is something incredibly satisfying about hand to hand combat. Without weapons getting in the way, it lets adversaries fight each other the way they were meant to. Winning takes speed, strength, agility, and brains, and it requires you to summon inner strength you may not have realized you had. That being said, there's such a thing as too much of a good thing.

I tossed another wolf across the otherwise deserted street. If the witches hadn't already earned their keep for The Society, they did that night. There's no way we could have cleaned up that kind of chaos without messing with human minds. I'm not sure what people thought was happening, but clearly the growling and screaming on the street wasn't garnering any attention.

"You're actually kind of good at this," Jared yelled from somewhere behind me. Was it possible the guy had a sense of humor?

"Yeah. So are you."

He laughed. "I'm the best. Don't pretend you didn't know that."

"I figured the stories were inflated, like everything else about your breed."

"I'd love to hear those stories but it looks like we have more company."

I turned in time to watch another four bears barreling down the street. More grizzlies. Black bears were fairly easy, but the grizzlies were far worse. They had more upper body strength, and if you weren't careful, they'd knock you over before you could react. Lucky for me, Pterons have good reflexes and I'd managed not to get knocked around too much.

The bear who initiated the attack, and had the personal interest in Casey, disappeared sometime during the early waves of attacks when I didn't have the time to chase after him. I'd find him eventually, but until then, I had my hands full. I was glad to have Jared and Owen there. As strong as my men were, two extra well-trained Pterons wasn't something to scoff at.

As the bears approached, I flew sideways to dodge the head on attack. I swiftly rammed them from the side. Jared seemed to have the same idea. The bears were more vulnerable on their sides.

Reinforcements arrived right as the fourth round of bears and wolves appeared. I nodded in greeting to Tom and Tim. It was about time they got their asses there.

We took down that line and another before the meek shifters realized the futility of a continued fight. The wolves retreated first, with the bears on their heels. I sent Tim and Tom after them. I'd let them take care of the low lifes.

"Do you think our friend here is ready to talk?" Owen kicked the human body of a bear who had been there in the very beginning. He was the only one other than the ring leader who had survived from that first group.

"I don't know." Jared stepped closer to the body. "Let's find out." He stepped on the shifter's chest. "Are you ready to talk yet, asshole?"

Our prisoner grunted.

"In English please." Jared pushed his shoe in harder.

"Move. Foot." He struggled to talk.

Jared moved his foot. "Talk."

"Why should I?"

"Because you don't have a choice." I leaned down over him. "What do you want with the girl?" I didn't like describing Casey that way, but I wasn't using her name in that kind of company.

"You mean besides fucking her?" He grinned as best he could despite his busted face.

I got rid of the smile with my sneaker. "I'll ask you one more time."

He grunted. "It's our business, not yours."

"Everything is our business." Jared moved to his other side. We had him surrounded.

"Get ready for a new way of life. The Pterons are going down."

"Answer the damn question. Why the girl?"

"Because we want her." He swiped at me with a knife and drew blood in a line along my chest.

"You shouldn't have done that." Jared looked at me. "You think we're done here?"

I nodded.

"Good." Jared stepped on him again. "Take care of this piece of shit," he yelled at one of the Pterons starting in on the cleanup.

"You okay?" Jared asked, eying my wound.

"Yeah. A knife though? Who the hell uses a knife?"

"Weak shifters who don't have enough faith in their own strength." Owen spit on the body as we walked away.

"I need to see her." They knew exactly who I meant.

Jared nodded. "I'll catch up with you later. I need to check in with Levi."

"You don't have to come."

"You mean fighting shoulder to shoulder hasn't made us friends?" He smirked.

"No, it means I can stand you now."

"Yeah, I can say the same to you, but you should probably clean up that bad boy. Don't want to scare Casey with your war wound."

"I need to get an update from my cousins. After that, I'm going up."

"Suit yourself. Let me know if you run into any more trouble." Jared stuffed a hand in his pocket. He seemed completely unaffected by what we'd just done. I guess I probably seemed that way too.

"Oh, I will. I wouldn't want you to miss the fun."

"Keep that in mind when you see Casey." He winked and took off before I could respond.

"Asshole."

"I won't argue with you there. See you around." Owen took off after him.

I took one last glance at the carnage on the street before heading up to the sky myself. What a messed up night.

Chapter Eighteen

Casey

"This is Toby's house?" I looked out the car window at the Tudor style mansion. Surrounded by what had to be acres of property, it was the kind of place I couldn't imagine someone actually owning.

"It's his now." Cody yanked open my door. He reached toward me and I flinched.

"I'm not going to hurt you." He untied my legs and arms.

"You untied me?" I rubbed my wrists.

"Yeah. You're safe here. I wouldn't advise running off on your own, but if you really want to leave, you can."

I looked at him skeptically. It didn't make sense.

"Toby's going to get here as soon as he can, but he can't leave until he gets things in order."

"So what am I supposed to do until then?"

"Relax. There's a pretty extensive wine cellar. You can check that out."

I'm sure my jaw dropped. "You think I want to sit and drink wine after being kidnapped?"

"You weren't kidnapped. You were saved."

"I was tied up and thrown in the back seat of a car. That's kidnapping."

"I only did it so you wouldn't scream or try to run away. Those bears would have gotten you."

"Why should I believe you?" I tried to get all the kinks out of my body from sitting funny.

"Because you don't have a choice. You did something to get their attention, and they've already lost their minds. I wouldn't suggest spending time with insane shifters."

"What do you mean they've lost their minds?"

"They're attacking people in an attempt to get attention. That's asking for trouble. The king will have no choice but to retaliate and they know it."

"You keep talking about the king. Who is he?"

"He was the prince until a month ago. He's down in New Orleans with his new queen."

"Is she a Pteron too?"

He blanched. "No. Pterons don't mate with Pterons."

"What kind of shifter is she then?"

"She's human. We don't screw around with anyone else."

"Why would you mate with humans? Aren't we weaker?"

"We select the strongest. It keeps the gene pool fresh, and the Pteron gene is dominant so we don't have to worry."

"Do all shifters do that?"

He shrugged. "Some do. Some don't."

I hobbled over to the porch and sat down. My ankles were raw, and I had no idea where I was going. I wasn't running anywhere. I needed to see Toby. "Earlier…did you really mean it when you said Eric was a bear?"

"Yeah. He kind of looks like one, huh?" Cody smiled and he looked even younger.

"He is big…but why were you working as a doorman? And why the disguise?"

"I work security. Toby doesn't like to make it obvious he has someone watching his place."

"But you always know when he's in or not, right?"

"Yeah."

"So why did you send Jared up that morning?"

Cody smiled again. "Ah, I thought I'd buy Toby some time. I forgot you were still there. He didn't bother you, did he?" His body seemed to tense, and I sensed there was more that he wasn't saying.

"Why would you care?"

"Because Toby's made his intentions clear. No crow is touching you."

"His intentions clear? Crow?"

"I already told you that Toby likes you. I don't need to keep stoking your ego, do I?"

"So his intentions are of dating me?"

"Of mating with you…but you can call it that."

"Mating?"

"Yeah. We can date who we want, but we generally settle down with one person."

"Like marriage?"

"Yes."

"Toby doesn't want to marry me." We'd just started hanging out. A couple of intense kisses doesn't make a guy jump to thoughts of marriage.

"I'm not going to argue about this. It's really none of my business."

"Then tell me what you meant by crow?" I stretched out my legs on the step below me.

"We're hawks. Jared, as well as the king and his family, are crows."

"Is it random? The bird you're tied to?"

"No, it's not random." He scrunched up his face. "We tend to stay with our own."

"So Jared's in New York because..."

"The king sent him." Cody leaned against the railing. "He's the head of security."

"Jared?" My eyes probably bugged out. "He's practically my age, isn't he?"

"How old do you think the king is?"

"I don't know. Forty?"

"He's twenty-two."

"What?"

"He just took over for his dad. It's not a coincidence that the bears and wolves are pulling this crap. They think we're vulnerable."

"Who's we? I'm so confused." I rested my head in my hands.

"The Pterons run The Society. Not everyone's happy with that."

"Oh. That makes some sense. Why do you run it? No offense, but how do birds scare wolves and bears?"

"It's our hybrid form. We're stronger, faster, and smarter."

"Because you don't shift completely into birds?"

"Yeah."

"Why don't you?"

"Don't you know about Darwin's principles?"

"Evolution? Survival of the fittest?"

"Yeah. We evolved into the strongest form, and we reap the benefits."

"Sounds nice." How was I talking to this guy so calmly? Was he using some sort of power to keep me relaxed? I didn't understand it, and I was too exhausted to try.

"How are you feeling?" He kneeled down in front of me. "Want me to look at your cuts? I'm sorry if I hurt you."

I studied his face. He seemed genuinely concerned, but it could have been an act. I wasn't sure what I could believe. "You really thought it was the only way?"

"Yeah. Trust me. Toby's going to be pissed when he sees you. Hurting you isn't going to help me move up the chain."

I formulated more of my plan. "Maybe we can help each other."

"Help each other?" He looked at me warily.

"I need information. You give it, and I'll put in a good word." I wasn't sure if he was right about Toby caring, but I had to try.

"I've already given you information."

"I need more."

"Like?"

"If I wanted to find the bears, how would I?"

He coughed. "Why would you want to find them?"

"Why doesn't matter."

"Of course it does. I just dragged you up here to get you away from them. You know more than you're telling."

I crossed my arms. "They have something I want."

"Now the truth comes out. What the hell are you hiding?"

"None of your business."

"It is my business. We can't help you if we don't know what we're up against."

"You don't have to help me. You have enough to worry about with those attacks. I just need intel."

"Intel? Are you a spy or something?" He grinned, and I decided he wasn't quite as bad as I thought. "You know what your easiest solution is."

"What?" What obvious avenue was I missing?

"Eric. He's a bear."

"Yeah…but I don't know if I can trust him. Toby said he's dangerous."

"He is, but not if you're with us."

Did that mean he planned to continue helping me? "Well, he's not the bear I need."

"No, you just want the psycho ones that chase you through the Village."

"Exactly." I cracked a smile.

"What do they have of yours?" His expression softened.

"I can't tell you." Cody may not have tried to kill me or anything, but I certainly wasn't going to trust him with that kind of information.

"Can you tell Toby?"

"Maybe." I wanted to. I wanted to be able to tell him anything, but everything was still up in the air.

"Well, he'll be here soon. Let's go inside."'

"I feel better out here." I looked up at the dark sky.

"It could be hours."

"So?"

"So, we can't sit out here the whole time."

"Why not?" I felt much safer outside. The vast expanse of open grass calmed me. It also allowed for a much easier escape than being inside. Also, theoretically, someone could come to my rescue outside, if I needed rescuing.

"Mind if I go inside for a minute, then?" He paused with one foot on the step next to me.

"You'll leave me out here?"

"I'll be right back, and I already told you you're not being held against your will. Toby wants you to stay, but it's your choice."

"Where are you going?"

"To take a leak. I'd invite you, but Toby would probably get pissed."

"Pissed? That's almost a pun."

"And you're definitely different than I expected. I'll be right back." He took off his shirt, and two large, brown wings splayed out.

The wings looked almost exactly like Toby's, and I found myself unable to tear my eyes away. "What are you doing?"

"I don't have a key. I'll have to fly in the attic window."

"I'm never going to get used to this."

"Sure you will." He flew up to the attic, pushed open a window and disappeared inside.

I stared out at the yard, illuminated only by one small porch light, wondering what my next move should be. Was I being stupid to just sit around waiting for Toby, a guy I barely knew who had a pair of wings on his back? Did it make me certifiably insane that I still liked him, and kind of, sort of wanted to know what his wings would feel like under my hands?

A creaking sound had me up on my feet.

"Didn't mean to scare you." Cody, still shirtless, stood at the door. "Are you ready to come in?"

"I already told you I like it out here." The problem was once he brought up the bathroom, I had to go.

"You sure there's nothing you need to do inside?" He pulled his t-shirt back on over his head.

"Can you read minds?"

"No, but you're crossing your legs, and we were in the car for awhile."

"Promise not to try anything?" Not like that promise would mean anything, but I had to ask for it.

"If I wanted to hurt you, wouldn't I have done it already?"

"Maybe, maybe not. You could be waiting for reinforcements."

"Didn't you see how easy it was for me to get you in the car? I don't need reinforcements."

My bladder screamed at me. "Okay."

He held open the door, and I walked into a dark hallway. Lined with faded old pictures, it looked like it belonged in another time period.

"It's the third door on the left." Cody pointed in the direction of a hallway off the main one.

I nodded. "Thanks."

I walked down the hall tentatively, half convinced something was going to jump out and attack me. I had just discovered that paranormal creatures existed after all. And I'd kissed one. I'd kissed a paranormal creature. That meant he wasn't human. The scary part was he wasn't the first non-human I'd kissed. Chances were good that Murphy's brother wasn't human either. And I'd done a whole lot more than kiss him.

I found the bathroom, happy to discover it appeared to be something out of the twenty-first century. I took my time, not sure I wanted to face any more of the craziness. My nerves were fried, and I felt near my breaking point. I also didn't want to face the growing feeling that I had something to do with the attacks. It didn't make any sense, but why take Vera, and then go after me?

I wanted Toby. The thought came suddenly, and I splashed water on my face to make it go away. Using Toby for information was one thing, but did I really still want someone who wasn't human? Yes. The answer gnawed at me. I kind of wanted him more, and that was a really scary thought.

"Casey? Are you okay?" Cody called. It sounded like he was right outside the door.

"Yeah. I'll be right out." I splashed another round of water on my face and patted it dry. I tied my hair up in an attempt to make myself look more like a strong survivor than a disheveled victim.

"Take your time. I was just checking." He sounded embarrassed. I doubt he wanted to ask. Maybe he was afraid I was crying, or even worse, that I needed a tampon or something. Cody seemed like the kind of guy who'd get freaked out over that.

"Thanks."

"I'm going to see if there's anything edible in the kitchen."

I waited for his footsteps to disappear down the hall before opening the door. It's always weird to open a door when someone's right there.

I heard talking and followed it to the kitchen. Cody was on the phone. "So we should plan to spend the night, then?"

My stomach churned. That didn't sound good. I waited just outside the entryway.

"He's going to be okay though, right? I don't think we can handle another power switch."

"Is he okay?" I stepped into the kitchen, giving away my eavesdropping. I hoped by some chance he wasn't talking about Toby.

Cody held the phone away from his ear. "He'll be fine." He returned to the call. "I've got to go." He hung up.

"What happened to Toby?"

Cody swallowed hard. "He's going to be okay."

"Tell me." I gripped the counter.

"He got a little cut, that's all."

A cut? I was positive it was a lot bigger than that. "Is he coming here?"

"Yeah. He's taking care of some things, but then he'll head up."

"Soon?"

Cody smiled. "Toby would be glad to see your concern. The flight won't take long, but he can't leave yet. Let's find something to eat, and then you can get some sleep while you wait."

"Get some sleep? Are you kidding me?"

He opened the cabinets and pulled out a jar of peanut butter and some crackers. I picked them up and checked the dates. They both were well within expiration—impressive for a house that didn't seem to be frequently used.

"Sleeping is usually advisable." He spread a thick layer of peanut butter on a couple crackers.

"Yet not necessarily possible." I knew a lot about sleepless nights. I had them more often than not.

"You're safe here."

"Clearly, I trust you. I'm inside the house, standing here calmly while you wield a knife."

He chuckled. "Wield a knife? I'd worry more about my pinky than a butter knife."

"Yeah, that was a joke, and your response didn't exactly put me at ease."

He bit into a cracker. I wondered if Pteron teeth were stronger too. "You're only stuck with me for a few more hours."

"Good to know."

He laughed again. "I wonder if that's what Toby sees in you. I mean, besides what you look like."

"What do you mean?"

"You're funny. You've got this wittiness to you that you probably don't even realize you have."

I reached over him and dipped a cracker in the peanut butter. I preferred crunchy, but creamy was better than nothing. I didn't bother with a knife.

"Toby barely knows me."

"Yet you've been staying at his place…"

"In the guest room."

"Sure, the 'guest room.'" He made air quotes. His skepticism reminded me of Jared. I wondered where he fit into all of it. Was he still in New York with Toby?

"I'm not sleeping with him."

"Maybe not yet, but it's inevitable. I saw the way you reacted when you thought he was hurt."

"Caring about someone doesn't mean you want to sleep with them."

"It does in your case. You were about to be mauled by a bear but you were more concerned with staring at him without a shirt on."

"Was not."

"Were too." He opened another sleeve of crackers.

"We sound like children."

"Yes, we do." He stuffed two crackers in his mouth.

I nabbed one more. "I still can't believe any of this."

"It's about to get even more real." He leaned up against the counter.

"Why's that?"

"Toby's here."

"Where?" I walked to the doorway and looked down the long, empty hallway. Satisfied there was no one there, I walked back over to Cody.

Cody smiled. "I heard him land. He'll be in soon."

Chapter Nineteen

Toby

I pushed open the front door. "Casey?" I sensed movement in the kitchen and walked right in.

She gazed at me for half a second, as if deliberating, before running into my arms. I held her close, even more relieved to see her than I expected.

I patted her back. I needed to find a way to offer comfort without coming on too strong.

She buried her face in my bare chest. It felt right. "Are you hurt?"

"No. I'm good."

"Are you sure?" She lifted her head to look at me. There was such concern in her eyes. Concern for me. She ran her hand over the cut on my chest that was already starting to heal. There were a lot of benefits of being a Pteron.

"I appreciate the concern, but I'm fine." I put my hands on her arms and looked into her eyes. "What about you? Are you all right?" I gently touched the area around a faint cut on her forehead.

"Yeah, I'm fine." Her words sounded fake, and I needed to get to the bottom of it.

"I'm going to go watch the house." Cody touched Casey's arm as he squeezed by us to get to the door.

I swallowed down my annoyance at seeing anyone else touch her. "Thanks, man. I owe you." I wasn't sure if he had anything to do with the cut, but if it was unavoidable in order to get her away from the bear, I could let it slide.

"Just doing my job. Besides, I had some decent company." He winked at her. He was lucky I'd already done enough fighting that night.

She smiled. "And you're not so bad when you aren't kidnapping me."

"Kidnapped? Is that what you think?" My body tensed.

"Chill out. She's kidding. We're okay now."

"Good." In all the craziness of the night, I hadn't worried about whether she thought we were on the same side.

"I need to talk to you." Her words were soft, but I'm sure Cody could still hear them from the other side of the door.

I nodded. "Let's talk."

I led her into one of the formal sitting rooms. It was one of those rooms that served no purpose. What's the point of a room filled with uncomfortable furniture? I loved the location of the house, but if I ever moved in, I'd have to gut the place and turn it into something more modern. I pictured asking Casey to move in there. If I gave her the choice, she'd probably want to knock down the walls and revamp the outdated kitchen.

She took a seat on a brown sofa, and I sat down next to her, leaving less than the socially acceptable amount of space. I wanted to be close. She seemed unconcerned with discovering I had wings, but maybe that was just shock. I wasn't looking forward to the questions I knew were coming. "What do you want to talk about?"

"I know why the bears want me." She looked down, but that wasn't going to work.

I put a hand under her chin and lifted it up. "Why?"

"Well, I guess I don't know why, but I'm not surprised now that I know who they are. Oh, this is coming out wrong." She let out a breath. "Let's try it again."

I picked up her hand and held it in mine. It was so small and fragile, it looked like the kind of hand that needed to be held and kept safe, but I knew better. Casey was strong, she was a fighter. You could tell just by being in the same room as her. "I'm listening."

"They have my sister."

"The bears?"

"Yes. Murphy, that burly, creepy guy that you punched."

"Yes?"

"He was my sister's boyfriend and then she disappeared." Tears welled in her eyes, and I had to reach out for her.

I pulled her into my arms. "I'm sorry, Casey. Did he say anything about her?" I wanted to react, to do something, but staying calm was the only way I'd get more information from her.

"He said he'd take me to her. He wanted me to go with him. Eric told me to run."

"Would you have gone?" I watched her closely. How desperate was she to find her sister?

"Maybe."

My chest clenched at the thought of her willingly turning herself over to them. Still, I understand it. I knew the lengths someone would go to protect the people they loved. "How long ago did she disappear?"

"Two years ago."

"Did you know what Murphy was?"

She shook her head. "No. I had no clue. I introduced her to him because I was dating his little brother."

"You dated a bear…" I tried to keep the emotion out of my voice.

"Yeah, I guess so. We dated for a few months."

"Oh." I sensed there was more, a lot more, than she was saying. "We'll find her." We would. If it was what Casey needed, I'd get it done. She'd brought me more happiness in the few days we'd spent together than I'd had in months. I'd make things right for her. The only thing I feared was that the sister wouldn't want to be found.

She nodded. "Thank you."

"I have to clamp down on the violence. We took care of the majority of it, but there is likely more to come. After that, we find her."

"What if they're related?"

"Related?"

"Yeah. What if the reason they took her and why they want me is all related to the attacks. I mean, they can't be that desperate for girls."

"Did you just crack a joke?"

She smiled slightly.

Unbelievable. This girl was perfect.

"Sorry, I know I make jokes at bad times."

"Don't say sorry." I leaned in. "Don't ever say sorry."

I needed her lips, and I took them. I smashed mine into hers, wrapping her up tighter in my arms. I deepened the kiss immediately, pushing her to open up more. She moaned, clearly fine with the demand. Our tongues connected, and I was lost.

Without consciously thinking about it, I moved us so she was lying down with me hovering over her. She wrapped her arms around my neck, pulling me down on top of her. It was her turn to be demanding. Her nails raked up my back, and I needed more of her. I slipped a hand up her leg, letting it rest just below her ass as my other hand moved under her long sleeve shirt.

"Toby," she moaned as I let my lips wander down to her neck.

I heard someone clearing their throat, but I ignored it. Cody could get lost. I needed Casey, and she needed me.

"Well, hello there," a taunting voice said from the doorway.

I groaned, moving off Casey.

I took a moment to compose myself. "What the hell are you doing here, Florence?"

Jared smirked. "Obviously interrupting something good. Glad you two found a good use for this hideous couch."

His eyes zeroed in on Casey, and I belatedly realized I'd left her skirt and shirt riding up.

She fixed them before I could, and she looked incredibly embarrassed.

"How did you get in here?"

"Your friend let me in."

"Shouldn't you be on your way to New Orleans to brief the king?"

"I told you I'd be coming. Besides, I've got some news." He still watched Casey and that made me want to send him flying out of the room. I wasn't playing games. He wasn't going to screw things up for us.

"What kind of news?" I asked, knowing I wouldn't like the answer.

"He's coming here." Jared's smile got bigger.

"Fantastic." That was one way to kill a hard-on.

Chapter Twenty

Jared

So much for being his innocent house guest. Walking in on them shouldn't have bothered me that much, but it did. If he hadn't rolled off her, I probably would have thrown him across the room. There was something incredibly satisfying about ruining their moment, and I didn't miss the flush of red that crossed her cheeks when she realized they'd been caught.

"He's on his way now." I talked to Toby but kept my eyes fixed on Casey. From the glimpse of her stomach and thigh, I knew that her natural skin tone was a little bit lighter. I wondered if she'd gone away to get the tan. She didn't look like the type to fake-bake.

Toby looked at Casey apologetically. "I have to take care of a few things before the king gets here. What can I do to make you more comfortable while you wait?"

"I'll make her comfortable." I grinned at her, satisfied to watch her blush again. I liked being the one to cause it.

"No, that won't be necessary." He watched her, probably out of fear that he'd see some interest.

"I'll just wait here." She said it carefully, like she was afraid of conveying any sign of what she actually wanted.

"I'll keep you company." I sat down on the opposite side of the couch from where she sat as straight as an arrow.

She tugged down on her skirt, trying to make the fabric magically longer. "I can keep myself company."

"Go get ready, Toby. She's in good hands." I scooted over slightly and put an arm around the back of the couch.

Toby groaned, and I tried to maintain a straight face. "I'll be back in a few minutes."

I waited for him to leave the room before turning to look at her. "Why hello, sleep over girl. Or should I call you Casey? Nice to see you again."

She frowned. "Is it really nice?"

I didn't like the frown. I needed to fix it. "It is, although I'm a little disappointed."

"Disappointed?"

"That you misled me. I thought you were a single woman who happened to stay over at her friend's house."

"I stayed in his guest room."

"But was it really a friend's guest room?"

"Yes. No. I don't know." She crossed her arms. "Just drop it."

"I'm just looking for a straight answer. Are you, or aren't you with Toby?" I was asking to mess with her, but I actually cared about the answer.

"Maybe."

"You don't know?"

"Listen, Jared. That's your name, isn't it?"

"Yes. Glad you remember it."

"Whatever. I just survived a bear attack and found out that you guys have wings. Excuse me if I'm not forthcoming with answers about my love life."

In my state of annoyance over seeing her with Toby, I hadn't thought about the significance of her knowing who we were.

"And you're okay hooking up with us anyway?"

"First of all, I'm not hooking up with you, and second of all, we weren't hooking up. We were kissing."

"Kissing horizontally with his hands underneath your clothes. I was maybe five minutes early for the fireworks. Maybe ten if Toby's decent with some foreplay."

"Ugh. Shut up. We are not discussing this." She blushed again, and she couldn't hide how flustered I was making her.

"Why not?" I brushed my fingertips against the back of her neck.

She flinched but then leaned back into my hand. Interesting.

"Because I don't discuss this kind of thing with random people."

"Didn't we just establish I'm not a person?" God, it was fun to push her buttons.

She stood up and turned to me. "Is this fun for you?"

"Is what fun?"

"Messing with me."

"Kind of."

"You're an asshole. A huge asshole who I don't appreciate. Just leave me alone."

"A huge asshole, as compared to a small one?"

"ARRGH!" She stomped her foot. She actually stomped one of her pretty, painted toenailed feet.

"Calm down. I'm just trying to distract you."

"Distract me?" She crossed her arms again, bringing my eyes to her chest. She was probably a full C cup, perfect.

"Yes. Distract you from everything else going on. You seemed stressed."

"I wonder why?"

"Wait. Are you suggesting I'm the one stressing you out? It wasn't the bear, or Toby, or anyone else?"

"Toby saved me. He and Cody."

"Cody? You mean that kid outside?"

"Kid?"

"Yeah. He's barely out of diapers." He was probably nineteen, but I might as well hurt the potential competition. She might have some savior syndrome going on.

"I don't care about his age."

"So you go for younger guys?"

"I'm not going for him," she said through clenched teeth.

Evidently, I'd pushed things too far. "Look, I'm sorry if we're getting off on the wrong foot."

"The wrong foot. Talk about the worst foot that ever existed." A small smile slipped out.

"Did you get anything to eat?"

"What is it with you guys and making sure I'm fed?"

"Who else asked?"

"Cody."

"Did he find you anything?"

"Peanut butter and crackers."

"There's got to be something better. Let's check it out." I hoped she accepted the olive branch.

"Sure." She turned away, and I knew she was trying to regain her composure.

We walked down the hall to the small kitchen. I searched the pantry, and came up mostly empty except for a box of pancake mix that you only had to add water to. "These aren't going to be great, but want some?"

She took the box from me. "Yes."

"I guess you are hungry."

"Uh huh. So why don't you take care of my dietary needs."

I wanted to tell her that I'd prefer to take care of some other needs first, but I didn't. I wanted this girl to like me—somehow it mattered. "Check out the upper cabinets for a measuring cup and bowl. I'll look for a pan."

"On it." She smiled again, and I felt kind of triumphant. It was the feeling I usually only got when I was about to get a girl in bed.

We spent the next half-hour cooking up pancakes. Casey insisted on making the whole box since Toby and Cody had to eat too. I decided not to remind her that there would be even more people showing up.

I convinced her we didn't need to wait for the others, and after discovering some syrup, we sat down to eat.

I heard conversation outside, so I polished off my plate. Casey was still eating when we heard their voices in the hall. She set down her fork and jumped out of her chair. I washed off our plates and took her hand. "Relax. They don't bite."

I was still holding her hand when Levi and Allie walked into the room.

Levi grinned when he saw the small hand I held in my own. "You're always good at making new friends."

I laughed, and Casey tugged her hand from mine.

Allie pushed him. "Be polite." She strode toward Casey. "Hey, I'm Allie."

"Allie? As in Toby's Allie?"

She looked at me funny and smiled at Levi. He didn't enjoy that comment. "Usually, people call me Levi's Allie, but I was at one point."

"Oh. Sorry. I guess you're the queen?" She mumbled a bunch of words in such a cute and dorky way.

"Casey, this is Allie Davis, soon to be Allie Laurent. She is the Queen of The Society, and this is her king, Levi."

Casey did some sort of half curtsey thing. "Pleasure to meet you."

Levi held out a hand to her. "Nice to meet you, Casey."

I answered Levi's questioning look. "Toby had her brought here for safe keeping."

"I figured she knew Toby."

"Yeah. I was chased by a bear..." she started to explain.

"Is Jared taking good care of you?" Levi asked.

"Uh yeah. We made pancakes."

"Jared isn't taking care of her." Toby walked in. "Good to see you Levi. Allie." He walked right over to Casey, putting an arm around her. I didn't miss the way she leaned into his side.

"So you're with Toby?" Allie looked between all of us.

"Yes." Toby ran his hand over her back. "Casey's with me."

"Yet she was making pancakes with Jared." Levi smiled. He liked to stir up trouble, like me.

"You really like making pancakes, don't you, Jared?" Allie teased. I did have a habit of making them at weird times.

"I need to use the restroom." Casey skirted out of the room.

"Leave Casey alone." Toby looked at both Levi and I when he spoke. He still hadn't made eye contact with Allie.

"She seems nice." Allie smiled. She was trying to ease the situation. She probably also felt for the girl. She of all people knew how hard it was to be a human pulled into the Pteron world.

"She is." Toby snuck a glance at Allie.

"I'm going to see if she's okay." Allie patted Levi's arm before walking out of the room.

Toby leaned in to me. "Stay away from her."

"Why?"

"Because she doesn't need you messing with her."

"Yet she needs you to do it?"

"I'm not messing with her."

I found a bottle of water in the fridge and opened it. "No, you're just confusing her."

"Excuse me?"

"She doesn't even know if you guys are together."

"We are."

Levi laughed. "Popular girl."

Toby ignored his comment. "I lost Allie, I'm not losing her."

I paused with the bottle of water midway to my mouth. "Whoa. Are you really going to go there?"

"Just stay away from her, Florence."

"You'd only say that if you thought she might want me."

"Just shut up. Levi isn't here to talk about this."

"No. I'm not." Levi gave me a look that would have made anyone shut up. "Where can we talk privately?"

"There's an office down this way," Toby led us into the hall. I could hear Allie talking with Casey quietly in the bathroom. Allie was a cool girl. Hopefully she'd put Casey at ease. No matter what happened to her, I doubted her life would ever go back to completely normal.

Chapter Twenty-One

Casey

Mortification took on a new meaning. I had no clue how to greet the king and queen, and now they thought I was messing around with two guys? Admittedly, they weren't my king and queen, but I still felt like a total screw up.

"Casey? Are you all right?" Allie called from outside the bathroom door. That was the second time that day someone had checked on me like that. I didn't enjoy it.

"I'm fine."

"Can I come in?"

My first thought was to send her way, but that would have just made things worse. "Sure. Come in."

She opened the door slowly, taking a seat on the edge of the tub. "Crazy, huh?"

She spoke so casually, and it immediately put me at ease.

"Yeah. Crazy is a good word for it."

"Have you known Toby long?" She seemed to be asking in order to make conversation rather than because she wanted to pry. It reminded me that she was his ex-girlfriend. The one who'd left him heartbroken somehow.

"I've served him coffee for months, but we only started hanging out this week."

She smiled lightly. "He's a nice guy."

"You dated him." I didn't bother phrasing it as a question.

"In high school. It just didn't work out."

"Yeah…was it mutual?"

"The breakup? No. He took it kind of rough." She wasn't gloating, and I was glad to see it. I liked her, and that would have made any semblance of a friendship impossible.

"About that…"

"Yes?"

"Why do your friends think he dumped you? Did you let him save face or something?"

Her face scrunched up. "What friends said that?"

"Jess and Emmett."

"You know Jess?" A puzzled look crossed her face. "She knows I'm the one who broke up with him."

"She said it was the opposite, but it doesn't matter."

"I guess not…" She seemed to think on it for a second. "But back to the here and now. How'd you end up at this house?"

"I was being chased by a bear."

"Ah. It's dangerous to be around these guys."

"I think the bear would have found me anyway." I don't know why I was so forthcoming with information, but she seemed like someone I could trust. Maybe it was the comfort of girl talk after hours of being with just boys.

"A good rule of thumb is that even if trouble would find you anyway, it's still their fault. It's more satisfying to view things that way." She smiled, and I could tell she was kidding. I could also tell she had her own crazy story to tell.

Cody had already answered the question, but I wanted to hear it with my own ears. "Are you completely…well…"

"Human?"

"Yeah."

"Yes. I'm human, and if Toby and Jared are both vying for you, I'm pretty sure you're human too."

"They're not both vying for me. Anyway, they really only date humans?"

She laughed. "They are. It's cute to see Jared that way. And yeah, it's a weird Pteron thing."

"Was it hard to get used to all this?" I spread my arms, but I assumed she knew I wasn't referring to the bathroom.

"Very. I ran from it quite a few times, but my situation was different."

"Did you freak when Toby showed you his wings?" Thinking about his wings was less frightening than I'd expected. I was more curious than anything, which was strange. I would have thought I'd be afraid.

"I saw Levi's first." She laughed. "Okay, that sounds kind of bad. Let's be more specific. I saw Levi's wings first."

"Did you know Toby wasn't human when you dated?"

"Not at all. I didn't find out until I was already with Levi." She shook her head, displacing some long, brown hair from her shoulder. Allie was gorgeous with big green eyes situated in a face that could definitely be defined as classically beautiful. She probably could have had a career in modeling. I tried not to let that intimidate me any more than her title already did.

"Oh. That must have been crazy to hear."

"Tell me about it." She tilted her head slightly.

"I'm sorry I ran off like that. I'm just not sure how to act. I mean you're a queen and I'm crying all over the place."

She laughed again. "Yeah, I'm a queen, but I'm also a nineteen-year-old college student. Don't sweat it."

"So what now?"

"Now we get out of the bathroom and grill the boys about what's going on. I hate being left in the dark."

"All right. Sounds like a plan."

I followed Allie out of the bathroom and down another hallway. She listened at the door for a second.

"You can come in," someone called from inside.

"I hate your super hearing." Allie pouted before taking a seat on Levi's lap. There were no empty chairs so I just stayed in the doorway.

"You can sit with me." Jared smirked. I wanted to make a smart ass comment back, but I'd already embarrassed myself once.

"Here, take my seat." Toby vacated the chair behind a heavy wooden desk.

"That's okay."

"I insist." He took a seat on the desk.

"Thanks." I sat down in the leather chair.

"What did we miss?" Allie didn't wait a beat.

"All right, let's see." Levi adjusted her on his lap. "Last night, we successfully took out the largest contingent of bears in the city, but some escaped. Combine that with the mumblings of similar uprisings in other regions, and the confirmed attacks in LA, and—"

Allie put a hand on Levi's leg. "Wait, attacks in LA? That's Cade's territory. Does he know?"

"Yes, babe. I'm well aware that you gave LA to Cade. We spoke a few minutes ago." Levi's response was laced with some slight annoyance, but he didn't seem particularly upset. I wondered who Cade was and how Allie could give him a major city.

"What are we going to do?" She turned so she could look at him.

"We're going to be ready for the attacks. We're going to take everyone, and we're going to break the prisoners we're holding."

"Prisoners?" I asked. I wasn't good at staying quiet.

"Yes. We took some last night."

"And then there's Bryant," Jared said quietly.

I looked around questioningly. "Who's that?"

"My brother." Jared stood up like he was ready to leave.

"What does he have to do with this?"

Toby turned to me. "Our informant said he'd tell us what we need to know."

"Your informant?"

"Marv..."

"Oh." Of course. Jared's brother, my boss, everyone was connected.

"Toby, I want you down in New Orleans with us. From Jared's briefing, Marv only responded to you. We may need his cooperation."

"Fine. I just need to set up some security for Casey."

"Can I come?" The words flew out of my mouth without thinking. Had I just invited myself on a paranormal reconnaissance mission?

"You want to come?" Toby asked. "You really don't have to."

"Have you ever been to New Orleans?" Jared asked from the doorway.

"No."

"Then she's coming." Allie hopped off Levi's lap. "Besides, that way I can introduce her to Hailey and everyone."

I had no idea who Hailey and everyone was, but I appreciated her enthusiasm.

"She'd be safer there." Levi looked at both Toby and Jared for an answer. I guess he was deferring the decision to them. I wondered why Jared had any say in it.

"I say yes. She'll enjoy the experience." The twinkle in Jared's eye made me wonder if he meant the city or spending time with him.

"I'd prefer to keep her close anyway." Toby smiled at me. "If that's okay with you."

"It's more than okay." If our kissing earlier hadn't made that clear, I didn't know what would.

"Good."

"I'm guessing you don't want Casey's first flight to be that long." Levi stood up, reminding me of just how intimidating he was. He even *looked* powerful. "I have the jet waiting, or you could take your own plane."

"We'll take our own. We'll have to fly back on our own in a few days."

Jared smiled at me. "Maybe I'll join you guys. See if the Blackwell's air digs are as nice as the Laurents'."

Levi and Allie exchanged a glance. "Sorry to ruin your fun, Jared. But you're flying yourself. I need you handling things for our visit to Bryant."

"Fine." He strode over to the desk, leaning around Toby to look at me. "See you soon, Casey. Have a nice flight." He winked before walking out of the room.

Toby took my hand. "I'll have the plane waiting for us. If you want to shower, feel free. I'll leave your bag outside the door."

"My bag?" I stood up.

"I packed a few things for you before I headed up here."

I stepped back. "You went into my home and packed some of my clothes?"

Levi laughed. "This is so much better when I'm not the one getting berated."

"I'm going to save you both from wasting the time and energy of having a fight." Allie turned to me. "Toby shouldn't have gone in your room and touched your stuff without permission, but he probably thought he was being thoughtful."

"I did, I just wanted you to—"

Allie held up a finger. "And Toby, you shouldn't have done it without permission, but I'm sure Casey will appreciate having something to wear. That is, if you packed decent stuff."

"Decent stuff?"

"If it's all sexy lingerie, I'll help her get you back."

Toby smiled. "I'm pretty sure I packed reasonably, and I tried not to spend too much time in your underwear drawer."

"Good."

After saying goodbye to everyone, mostly Allie, I made my third trip to that same bathroom. I locked the door and checked it twice before getting undressed and under the spraying water. The warm water washed away some of the grit of the day, and it woke me up. I reluctantly turned off the water and stepped out of the steamy stall.

Wrapped in a decently soft towel, I unzipped the duffel bag. Toby had done well. I pulled out a pair of jeans and a t-shirt as well as some fresh underwear. He'd grabbed a few cotton pairs, and I appreciated it.

One thing Toby didn't pack was a brush, so I attempted to use my fingers to straighten out the tangled strands. I searched through my purse and thankfully found an old hair tie and quickly pulled my hair up into a messy bun.

The house was quiet, but I thought I heard water running in the kitchen. I slowly walked down the hallway and took a moment to study the pictures on the wall. Most of them were portraits of people, but there were several landscape paintings mixed in. I walked the rest of the way to the kitchen.

"Feel better?" Toby asked. He was washing off the left over pancake dishes.

"Sorry about that."

"The dishes? Don't be. I'm glad you ate."

"Did you eat?" I knew how little food was in the house, and I had a feeling he hadn't stopped to eat before leaving the city.

"Yeah, I reheated some of the pancakes."

"Did they taste okay?"

"They were fine." He rinsed off the remaining dish and turned to me. "Did I pack all right?"

"Yes. Thank you." I wasn't going to mention a missing hairbrush when I'd already been mad at him for being in my stuff at all.

"Everyone else went ahead. If you're ready, we can go." He sounded eager, and I wasn't sure if it was to get down to New Orleans or to get out of the house. He didn't seem to be a big fan of the place.

"I'm ready."

Toby picked up my duffel and another bag sitting by the front door. I assumed that was full of his stuff. I wasn't sure how he flew with them, but I didn't need to know.

He locked up the house behind us and then opened the back seat of the car. After tossing in our bags, he opened the passenger door for me. I always liked when a guy did that. I was all about dating a gentleman—even if he also happened to have wings.

***

Like most people, I'd never been on a private jet before. I associated them with individuals who had way too much extra money. The thought of flying on one left me with a mix of nerves and excitement.

We pulled into the small airport, and I tried to choke down my nerves. They weren't going to help me. I had no one to blame for my current position. Toby seemed more than happy to let me go back to the city with some protection, but that wouldn't get me closer to Vera. Delusional or not, I was convinced that sticking close to the Pterons would give me safer access to the bears, and a fighting chance of getting her back. Also, if Vera was tied in with the attacks, any information they found might help me.

"Are there going to be more passengers?" I asked as Toby led me down the tarmac.

"Why? Are you afraid of being alone with me?" he teased.

"No." I quickly brushed off the suggestion I knew was in his words. "I'm just wondering."

"Marv and my assistant are coming."

"Who's your assistant?"

"Nelly."

I pictured Nelly as a knock out blonde with perky breasts and perfectly white teeth. Although I didn't have much to go on when imagining what the executive assistant for a paranormal leader would look like. "Oh. Okay."

"I wanted her to come so I'd have more time to spend with you." He rested his hand on the small of my back.

"Really?"

"Why do you sound so surprised?"

"Because with everything else going on, are you really worried about spending time with me?"

He didn't hesitate with his answer. "Yes."

I smiled, taking big steps to keep up with his pace.

We boarded the plane, and the first thing I noticed was Marv sitting next to a dark haired woman. Even seated, I could tell she was petite and she smiled at me lightly as we approached.

She stood up and shook my hand. "You must be, Casey. Toby's told me so much about you."

I glanced at Toby.

He took my arm and gestured to the slight woman. "This is Nelly."

"You're Nelly?" She didn't fit my image at all. "Hi, Marv." I belatedly greeted my boss. I wasn't sure what I thought about the fact that he was a bear. Did he really just randomly hire me? Did Murphy find me because of where I worked?

"Hi, Casey. I'm sorry you've been brought into all of this." His words sounded genuine.

"We should take a seat." Toby walked further back and waited for me to take the window seat. I buckled my seatbelt while he sat down. "Once we take off, we can move somewhere more comfortable."

"This is perfectly comfortable."

He smiled. "You are so low maintenance."

"As compared to?"

"I don't know…you just seem so easy for a girl." He seemed to think better about his word choice when he saw my face. "Not easy in that way, but easy going."

"Sure." I feigned offense, but I took it as a compliment.

"This should be a really short flight anyway."

I shifted in my seat. "But it should be enough time for you to answer more questions."

"Sure." He stretched out his long legs that were currently covered in jeans. He'd taken a break from the suits.

Given carte blanche to ask any question, I found I didn't feel like it. "Maybe later." I rested my head back and closed my eyes.

He laughed. "Okay, that was fast."

"Maybe asking questions isn't the answer. I kind of like the version of things I'm creating in my head."

"I'd love to see your version."

"Too bad you can't read minds."

"Yeah, too bad. I can see in the dark though, just so you know."

"That's cool…but why are you telling me?"

"Because I'm hoping that you eventually spend a lot of time in the dark with me, and I thought you should know I'll be able to see you." He put his arm around my shoulder just as we started taxiing.

I opened my eyes. "A lot of time alone in the dark, huh?"

"Yes. Maybe not today, but soon."

"How do you know I'm not a leave-the-lights-on type of girl?" I lowered my voice, hoping Marv and Nelly couldn't hear.

He leaned in. "That's fine with me, too."

"Would you mind if I napped?"

"Mind? Of course not."

"Okay, good." I leaned my head on Toby's shoulder and closed my eyes.

"Sleep well," he whispered against my ear.

"Don't go anywhere," I whispered back. As little as I knew him, he was my anchor in this crazy paranormal world. I wanted him close.

"I'll be right here." He rubbed my arm with his hand, and I eventually slipped off to sleep.

Chapter Twenty-Two

Toby

People sometimes confuse Pterons with angels if they catch a glimpse of us, but when Casey slept against my shoulder, she looked a heck of a lot more like an angel than I ever did.

Her breathing was even, and she looked so peaceful, although occasionally a troubled expression crossed her face. I hoped it wasn't a nightmare. Each time that happened, she tightened her hold on my shirt. I liked it. I wanted her to feel secure with me.

I'd been nervous about telling her what I actually was, but she'd taken it like a champ. If I wasn't imagining things, she seemed even more into me. That kiss back at the estate was epic, and I was definitely ready to discover more of her. I wasn't sure of the speed of how things would go with us, but she had a place in my life. If I needed to push other things out of the way to make room,

I'd do it in a heartbeat. I'd do a lot to be with her, and I was getting the sense she felt the same way.

"She's sweet," Nelly whispered from the aisle next to me. Standing up, she wasn't that much taller than me sitting.

"That she is."

"Marv was telling me she's a great employee too. Sounds like she understands hard work. I guess you two have a lot in common."

"Yeah? Because I'm such a hard worker?"

"You are. You just don't give yourself enough credit." She put a hand on my arm. "You really are incredible at what you do."

"Thanks." I tried to tactfully shrug off her hand. She was more of a touchy-feeling person than I'd prefer to have working for me, but she did her job well. "Hopefully Bryant has some answers. This better not be a wild goose chase." I knew Marv could hear me, and that was intentional. I wanted him to know there would be consequences if he was wasting our time. Even if I let it slide, Levi wouldn't. He had to use a strong arm to maintain his kingship.

"I put out a request for information on her." Nelly looked slightly guilty.

"Information? I didn't ask for any."

"I know, but I have to protect you. She could be lying about who she is."

"She works for Marv."

"Yeah, and look at how trustworthy he is."

Marv turned around in his seat to glare at Nelly.

"Anyway. I haven't heard anything back yet."

"Thanks, but no thanks." I wasn't going to sabotage our relationship that way. Casey would tell me what she wanted to tell me when she was ready. "Who'd you contact? I want you to cancel it."

She pursed her lips. "Are you sure that's a good idea?"

"Yes. I insist you cancel it."

She nodded. "You really like her."

"Yeah, I do."

"Then isn't a background check even more important?"

"I'll ask her about her past when the time is right."

"All right. I'll let you enjoy yourself." She patted me on the shoulder and walked back to the front.

I groaned internally. I didn't want to think about Casey having any kind of history. The last time I found out a girl I liked had history, it was to learn that Allie was like a magnet to any Pteron heir. That's how she ended up as queen. If Casey's history had anything to do with Jared's interest in her, I'd hurt someone. I wasn't losing another girl to a crow.

Casey snuggled further into my chest. She smiled and mumbled something resembling my name. It may have been something else, but I took it.

Casey slept the whole flight. So much for the questions she'd promised to throw my way. Hopefully, we'd have more than enough time to talk about them on our trip. I'd reserved us a two bedroom suite at the Crescent City Hotel. Booking a room at a hotel owned by Allie's dad felt weird, but it also housed the headquarters for The Society and was the safest place in the city. I hoped she didn't mind the presumption that she'd share a suite with me. I figured it wasn't all that different from staying in my apartment.

She didn't even wake up when we landed. I gently shook her and spoke quietly. "We're here."

"What?" she asked groggily.

"We're in New Orleans."

She opened her eyes, still resting her head on me. "Already?"

"Yeah. You were out cold."

"Did you sleep?"

"No." I decided not to fill her in on just how little sleep I needed.

"Oh. Sorry that I just abandoned you then."

I brushed some hair away from her face. "I was very comfortable."

Evidently, it was the wrong thing to say because she picked up her head and unbuckled her seatbelt. "What's the plan?"

"It's late. We're checking into the hotel."

"Hotel?" There was a note of nervousness in her voice.

"You have your own room, but it's in a suite with me. You'll be safe."

"I'm not worried." She let down the rest of her hair and ran her fingers through it before tying it back up. Her hair looked more wavy than usual and I wanted her to let it back down.

We didn't talk much when we deplaned and made the drive downtown. She still seemed sleepy, and I was happy to have her sitting next to me in the car. She waited quietly while I checked us in and we took the elevator up to our floor. Marv and Nelly decided to get a drink at the bar.

I pushed open the door to our suite and gestured for her to walk in first. "You can take either room."

"Oh, thanks. I'll take this one." She chose the one further from the door, the room I wanted her to take because I could protect her better that way.

"Great." I carried her duffel bag in for her.

"Believe it or not, I'm still tired." She leaned against the door frame.

"It was only a two and a half hour flight. You need more sleep than that."

"Are you going to sleep?" She yawned the cutest yawn I'd ever heard, but then she covered her mouth as though she'd done something embarrassing.

"Yeah. I'll get some sleep." I probably would get an hour or so.

I said good night and went into my bathroom to take a shower. I couldn't stop the thoughts of Casey that ran through my head as I stood under the hot water. She'd gotten under my skin, and I knew it wasn't going to get any better.

Dressed in just my boxers, I sat back on the bed. I picked up my phone and flipped through my emails. Nothing but work related ones waited for me.

I slipped into the sheets and closed my eyes. I'd need some sleep to deal with the circus of my life the next day. Levi was in charge, but I wasn't going to sit back and let him call all the shots.

A scream came from Casey's room and I sat up with a start. I ran to her room, pushing open her door within seconds of leaving my bed. I looked into the mostly dark room. She'd left the bathroom door ajar with a light on. She lay in bed with a look of absolute fear on her face.

"Toby?" She said my name softly, and it got me right in the heart.

"Yeah. I'm here." I sat down on her bed right next to her. I looked her over. She seemed physically fine, and I wondered if it were more nightmares.

"Did I scream out loud? Did I wake you up?"

"You screamed, but you didn't wake me up. Are you okay?"

She nodded. "But would…"

"Would I what?"

"Never mind."

I was pretty sure what she wanted, but if I was wrong I'd make a fool of myself. I went with it. "Do you want me to stay with you?"

"Yeah." She played with the sheet at her waist. She was wearing a tank top and a pair of shorts. Hopefully she didn't mind the sleeping attire I'd picked either.

"Of course." I stretched out next to her on top of the covers.

"No, you can come under. The fan is on and you'll get cold."

I could have assured her I wasn't going to get cold, but that would have involved turning down the opportunity to get into bed with her. I wasn't making that mistake again. I maneuvered under the sheets, keeping a small distance between us, not sure what she wanted.

"Thanks." She moved over, resting her head on my chest again. This time was different. This time I was nearly naked, and we were in bed together. It was intimate, something couples did, and I loved it. I wanted to know it wasn't a one-time thing, because going to sleep with Casey in my arms was perfect.

"If you want to talk about your dream, just let me know. But you don't have to." I didn't want to break the spell of comfort between us, but I wanted her to know she could tell me anything. I'd do anything for her. That realization hit me hard as I ran a hand gently down the bare section of her back that the tank top didn't cover.

"It's about my sister. I have it a lot."

I didn't push her any further. I just kept rubbing her back, hoping my presence and touch helped her fall asleep.

"I'm glad you know my name."

I smiled. "Yeah, me too. I've known it a long time though."

"I mean that you liked me too, and that my name mattered." She said it all sleepily, but I knew what she was getting at.

"I feel the same way about you having feelings for me. I thought you were just friendly to everyone."

"I've thought about this a lot." She ran her hand down my chest, and I never wanted her to stop touching me.

"About what?"

"Lying with you this way. I thought about it the first time I stayed over at your place."

"So did I." I'd also thought about it every night since.

"I can't believe I came down to New Orleans with you."

"Me either. It was a nice surprise."

"Thanks for letting me come."

"Of course. I wanted you here." I rubbed her back gently.

"Do you think we'll find my sister?" She sounded so sad it nearly broke my heart.

"I will do everything in my power to help you find her."

She smiled. "Thank you."

"Thank you."

"What are you thanking me for?"

"Making my life better." I kissed the top of her head.

"I hope that continues."

"Me too." My resistance was tested that night. Everything about her lured me in. Her scent, that sweet face, her warm body resting against mine—I loved it all. I couldn't ruin it. I couldn't push her if it wasn't what she wanted. If she needed to take things slow, I'd wait. I'd wait as long as I had to. In that moment, lying with her in my arms, I realized something. I was over Allie.

Chapter Twenty-Three

Jared

"They're twenty minutes late." I checked my watch for the third time. We'd been waiting in the lobby of the Crescent City Hotel for over twenty minutes, and so far Toby and Casey had failed to show.

"It's fine. An extra few minutes isn't going to kill us." Levi shrugged it off. Of course he did. He took everything calmly now that he had Allie. It's like they were on an extended honeymoon even though their wedding hadn't happened yet.

"It's just rude."

"Rude? Is Jared Florence really complaining about someone being rude?" Allie tore herself away from Levi's side long enough to get in my face.

"Yes."

Levi put his hands on her hips, pulling her back to lean against him. "No, it's because he wants to sleep with her."

"No." Allie groaned. "You're not allowed to go after Toby's girlfriend."

"Girlfriend? She's not his girlfriend."

"Says who?" Allie challenged with her words and eyes. One of Allie's best attributes was her tough as nails attitude. From what I knew of Casey so far, she had that trait too.

"Casey. She told me she wasn't with him."

"Maybe it's like me telling people I didn't really want to be with Levi…"

"We all knew that was crap." Levi grinned but he wasn't doing that when she played hard to get for months.

"Either way, leave her alone. She seems cool, and she doesn't need you messing with her." Allie got this pouty look I'm pretty sure she reserved for me.

"Why would I mess with her?"

"Using her and throwing her out counts as messing with."

"Using her? Who said I was going to use her?" I found the insinuation offensive. My reaction alone should have had me running the other way from Casey.

"I just mean she's not looking for a one-night stand. Let it go. Besides, she's definitely not your type. You just want her because she picked Toby instead."

"My type? And she didn't pick Toby over me."

Levi's phone rang. "Hi. Are you guys coming?" He smiled. "Okay, then. We'll see you in five."

"What?" I asked.

"They slept late…they'll be down soon."

Levi was accepting that as an excuse? "Haven't they heard of an alarm?"

"I don't think they were thinking about alarms." Allie smiled.

"What?"

"Come on, what do you think they've been doing?"

"No, thanks." I really didn't need to think about it. That girl deserved better. She actually had a sense of humor, and with a body like hers… I couldn't let my mind go there. I needed to stay in complete control if we were seeing Bryant.

I was about to suggest we leave to join Marv and Nelly for breakfast, when I saw Toby and Casey walking from the elevator, hand in hand. They kept stealing little glances at each other.

Allie laughed. "Yeah, we know what they were doing."

"Holding hands means they're having sex?" I was in no mood for Allie's analysis.

"No, but the looks they're giving each other does. And look at that glow. That's a post sex glow."

"Are you trying to piss me off?" I scowled at her.

Levi, of course, jumped in to defend her. "Back off, Jared."

They reached us, and I made myself appear unaffected. I should have been unaffected. Instead, I wanted to rip Toby's head off. If someone could read my mind at that moment, they probably would have had me restrained.

"Hey, Casey!" Allie grinned. "Did you sleep well?"

"Yeah. Very well." She looked around at the group, but when she reached me, she turned away.

That wasn't happening. "Oh yeah? Toby's snoring didn't keep you up?"

If they slept in separate rooms, she'd correct me and tell me she wouldn't know. "No. No snoring kept me up." An intimate look passed between the two of them.

Fuck. Allie was right. I shouldn't have cared, but I did. I wanted Casey, and I always got the girls I wanted. It's not like it was over. He may have had her first, but she wouldn't look back after a night with me. The trick was getting her alone long enough to set that up.

"Where are Nelly and Marv?" Toby asked.

"At breakfast in the dining room." Levi pointed to the entryway to the room.

"Did you guys eat?"

"No. I figure we can pick something up on the way. They were already ordering when we got here."

"Sounds fine to me."

"So, Casey, did you get a chance to see any of the city last night?" My eyes zeroed in on her face, she'd have to look up at me eventually.

"No. We came right here from the airport and it was already late." She looked up, and for a split second, our eyes met.

"That's too bad. I'll have to remedy that tonight. Let's plan on dinner at eight and go from there."

"We'll be back by then?" Nice, she hadn't completely shot me down.

"We'll be back tonight." Toby put his arm around her waist. "Where did you want to do dinner?"

"You weren't invited."

"I wasn't?" His smile said it all. He wasn't going to play dead and roll over. That just made it better.

"No. Casey's never been here. I'm giving her the special treatment."

"I heard your dad owns this place, Allie. It's gorgeous." Casey glanced around the lobby. Her eyes stopped on the chandelier with dangling crystals.

"I think so too. It's got a lot of character."

I couldn't resist that opening. "I'll show you lots of places with character..."

"You are a character, Jared." Allie nudged my shoulder.

I ignored Allie and focused all my attention on Casey. "I promise, Casey. It'll be a good time.

She bit her lip, and I knew I was in.

"Eight sound good?"

"Aren't we supposed to be visiting Bryant?" Toby interrupted before she could even answer.

Allie nodded. "We are. My Land Rover can seat everyone..."

I finally tore my eyes from Casey. "I'd call shot gun, but I'm guessing Levi's got that honor."

Allie shook her head. "No. He's driving. I'll take shot gun."

I laughed. "You still don't like driving it, do you?"

"Not when I don't have to."

"If you don't like the car, I'll take it." Casey smiled. She had this really pretty toothy smile. On some girls, it might have looked goofy, but it looked cute on her. It made you want to smile too.

Allie laughed. "I like it, but I prefer to let Levi do the driving. He complains the whole time when I do, and it's not worth it."

"Why are guys always like that?" Casey put her hand on her hip. "They are such back seat drivers."

"I know. It's definitely a gender thing."

I had to jump in. "I've known plenty girls who were backseat drivers."

"Do you know any guys who aren't if a girl is driving?" Casey asked.

"Specifically if a girl is driving?" I nodded my head in greeting when I caught sight of Nelly and Marv.

Casey held out one of her hands to the side. "Yeah. It's like when a woman is behind the wheel, the man thinks he's supposed to comment the whole time."

"You're not stereotyping at all, Case, huh?" Toby put his arm around her again.

Case? That was his nickname for her?

"Were y'all waiting on us?" Nelly tried to repress a smile.

"Don't go there, Nelly," Toby warned. I held in a laugh. It wasn't the first time a northerner tried to sound southern.

"What? I can't blend in?" She tried to look all innocent.

"Allie said it for the first time last week." Levi put a hand on her back.

"Yeah…I'm going local." Allie put her hands in the back pockets of her jeans.

I laughed. "Don't you mean loco?"

Levi punched my arm. "You did not go there."

I shrugged. "It's her fault."

Allie grinned. "Yes, I bring out his geeky side, and I'm proud of it."

"Jared has a geeky side?" Casey eyed me skeptically. "I can't imagine that."

"It's not so much geeky as it's being a loser," Levi taunted me.

Allie pulled out her cell phone. "Change of plans. We need two cars."

"Hailey and Owen?" Levi asked before I could.

"Yeah. She didn't want to miss the fun."

I cleared my throat. "Fun? Only Hailey would find a prison fun."

"I think she meant meeting Casey."

"Who's Hailey, and how does she know who I am?" Casey was funny. Sometimes she seemed so shy, but other times she'd speak her mind without a care.

"Hailey's my best friend and advisor. Her older brother, Owen, is Levi's advisor." Allie slipped her phone back in her purse. "And I told her about you."

Toby smiled. I wasn't sure why it made him happy unless he assumed she'd told everyone Casey was with him.

"Where are they?" I asked the obvious question. If they were together, they might as well just meet us at the prison. There was no point waiting for them to show up at the hotel.

"Behind you." Toby smiled like I'd said something stupid.

"Hey!" Allie hugged Hailey. Girls were funny that way. If they went two days without seeing each other, they'd hug like it had been years.

"Hey, long lost roommate." Hailey had her long, red hair pulled back into some sort of braid. I'd known her since she was in diapers, and she'd never worn it that way.

"I know! It's been a long few days."

"You must be, Casey!" Hailey walked right on over and shook Casey's hand.

The expression on Casey's face was priceless. "Uh, hi."

"Sorry. I'm just in a really good mood."

"Come on, Hailey. Casey was just attacked yesterday. Do you think she cares about your good mood?" I usually went into teasing older brother mode with Hailey. I guess it was a side effect of knowing her for so long.

"I care." Casey smiled. I wasn't sure if it was genuine or if it was an act to seem tough.

"I beat Owen at Foosball. I actually beat him!"

I laughed. "Seriously? Wow, are you getting lazy, man?"

"I don't think so. She's just that good now."

"That's awesome, Hail!" Allie hugged her again.

Casey looked at all of us questioningly. "Is Foosball a big deal for Pterons?"

Hailey laughed. "Not really, but beating my older brother is always satisfying, and blowing him away? Priceless."

Casey laughed. "I bet."

I wished I knew what was going on in her head. How did she really feel about hanging out with us? If she was sleeping with Toby, she couldn't be that freaked out, but maybe she'd freak out later. Allie had taken the revelation really well, but the girl Owen told flipped and moved across the country to get away from him. I was glad that, so far, Casey wasn't running. Of course, I would have to do something about the bed she was sleeping in.

After some discussion, I ended up in the backseat of Allie's Land Rover with Toby and Casey. Hailey drove everyone else in her jeep. I was nice enough to take the middle seat, although Toby didn't seem to appreciate the gesture.

We'd been on the road for about twenty minutes when Casey started in on the questions. I couldn't blame her, but man every question led to another.

"Why are we sure that Bryant knows anything? Do you guys trust Marv that much?"

"Ask Toby. He's the one who says we should."

"He's telling the truth." Toby leaned over me toward Casey. "Bryant knows something."

"And why do we think he's going to talk to us?" She looked away from me, like maybe she was afraid I didn't want to talk about my brother.

I took care of that concern. "My brother will talk if he's pissed off enough. He can't shut his mouth when he's mad."

Allie turned around from the passenger seat. "I'll second that, and he's scary when he's mad."

Levi put a hand on her leg. He still felt guilty that she'd been kidnapped by Bryant a few months earlier. I felt guilty too. It sucks having your flesh and blood turn out to be a traitor to your best friends.

I hoped Casey wouldn't follow up on Allie's comment. Hearing it again would just upset Levi, which would make the day that much worse. Levi was a royal pain—pun intended—when he was in a bad mood.

"Is Angola a state prison? Why do they let you keep your prisoners there? I mean, do they get the same trials and everything?"

"They don't let us keep our prisoners there, we let them keep theirs." Levi looked at her in the rearview mirror. She seemed nervous around him. Luckily, I didn't have that effect on her. Too bad I couldn't get another effect out of her.

"Oh. Do we need special clearance to get in?"

Toby reached over me to take her hand. "Don't worry. It's all taken care of."

What the hell was wrong with him? Did she want someone babying her like that?

"Angola Prison Rodeo?" Casey pointed at a sign. "It that for real?"

Allie turned in her seat again. "Uh huh. I've never been though."

"Do Pteron's participate?" Casey asked.

Levi turned off toward the first gate. "No, it wouldn't be a competition if they did. It's for humans only."

With such a large group, I expected we'd have to go through the normal security line, but luckily the guy running the check recognized Levi. He probably earned himself a fat raise by quickly ushering us through once we assured him none of us had weapons. We had no need for them. We were stronger using our own hands, and guns just seemed stupid. Where was the fun or skill in that?

We went down the stairwell that led us underground to The Society section of the prison. Instead of the regular prison guards, we used our own, and even I felt a little intimidated by the size of the men greeting us.

"Your majesty, we are honored to have you visit." The largest of the guards bowed his head slightly.

"Thank you. As we told you, we are here to see one prisoner in particular."

He nodded. "Yes. We have Mr. Florence ready."

My skin prickled. It was just another reminder that my brother had made such a stupid decision of where to put his loyalty. I hated hearing our family name associated with a prisoner.

Levi noticed my reaction and cast me the closest thing to an understanding look he had in his repertoire. I nodded and he turned back to the guard. "Let's see him then."

Toby pulled Casey off to the side and I listened in. "I don't think they're going to let you in the actual interrogation room."

Casey nodded nervously. "Okay. So I just wait outside?"

"I'm not going in either." Allie stopped, causing Levi to stop moving as well. "You can wait with me."

"Okay." Casey nodded again. I wouldn't have voiced it, but I was glad Toby wasn't even giving her a choice. Talking to Bryant would be hard enough without worrying about the stupid things he'd say to a couple of human girls.

In the end, only Levi, Marv, Toby and I went in. Owen wanted to, but Levi suggested he look out for the others, in other words, Allie.

Bryant was seated at a large rectangular table. With his hands and feet tied to the chair, he shouldn't have looked intimidating, but he did. There was just something about the set of my brother's jaw that made him appear as a force to be reckoned with.

"Oh, look at this. All my friends came over to play." His icy glare landed on me.

"Hello, brother." Two could play at that game.

"To what do I owe the honor of this visit?"

"Don't play dumb." Levi stepped closer to the table.

"I'm not playing at anything. They don't even give me toys here." He didn't need to say what toys he was referring to. I was glad the girls weren't in the room.

Bryant liked to brag about his sexual exploits, especially after Dad sent him to Europe because he fell for a Pteron. Dad's plan to get him away from the Pteron worked, but it also created a monster. Bryant had always been arrogant, but he came back something much worse.

"I already told them you're involved." Marv spoke for the first time since we'd arrived at the prison. His whole body was tense, and I could almost see the fear rolling off him.

"Did you? How thoughtful." Bryant sneered.

"They were going to find out anyway." Marv sounded a little more confident this time.

"Maybe, maybe not." Bryant turned his head to look at Levi. "The new king isn't exactly known for his brains."

Levi laughed. "And you are?"

"Even my idiot brother is smarter than you, Laurent."

"Is he?" Levi tried to hide a smile. He wasn't getting angry, and that in itself was impressive. Maybe Allie was rubbing off on him.

"Have you figured out why you needed an Enchantress yet?" Bryant referred to the title of what Allie was. An Enchantress was a human who had the power to pick the next Pteron king. Allie was the first one in several hundred years.

"Don't even think about Allie." Levi crossed his arms.

"I think about her a lot. She was the last girl I saw before getting thrown in here after all. Who else would I think about having wrapped around my dick?"

The table flew across the room and Levi had Bryant, still attached to the chair up against the wall. "Think you're funny, huh? Think you can talk about my queen that way? I have news for you, your life just got much shorter."

Toby inched toward Bryant too. I guess he did still care about Allie in his own way.

Levi dropped the chair. It fell backwards in the process and left Bryant sprawled on the floor.

"Is there a problem in here?" The guard tentatively stepped inside.

The girls all peeked in. Not smart.

"So you did bring me toys. Excellent. I'll take the taller one since Allie's already taken. She definitely looks like she'll provide some good entertainment." He licked his lips and Toby punched him in the face. I wanted to do the same thing, but Levi restrained me.

"No. No problem at all. We were just leaving." Levi kicked the remnants of the table as we turned our backs to Bryant.

"Leaving?" I gave Levi a disbelieving look. "We can't leave yet. We need answers."

"We'll get them. I know an expert at extracting information."

"Let me do it." I caught Levi's arm before he could leave the room.

"No. I can't expect you to torture your own brother."

"Levi, I can handle this."

"No. You can't. End of story." He stepped through the doorway.

Levi was wrong. Bryant was my brother. It was my job to get him to talk.

Chapter Twenty-Four

Casey

Toby left me alone in our hotel suite while he went to some meeting with Levi and a few others. I understood that I couldn't be included in everything, but I was antsy and refused to just sit around my hotel room while in a completely new city. I was willing to wait a while before venturing out, but I wasn't going to do it in my room. I'd noticed a bar in the lobby. It couldn't hurt to go down and order a drink or something.

I put on my boots and slipped my phone, room key, and a credit card in my pocket. After double checking that the door to our suite was locked, I took the elevator to the lobby.

There were a few people sitting at the bar, but I found an empty stool.

"Can I get you something?" a male bartender with dark hair asked.

"Just a Coke, please." I could use the caffeine and sugar.

"Sure. Coming right up." He filled a glass with ice and Coke then set it down in front of me.

I gave him my room number. Toby wouldn't mind me adding it to our room tab. I took a sip.

"Casey, hey!" Nelly smiled before taking the stool next to mine.

"Hey." Talk about good timing. I was glad to see a familiar face and a reminder that I wasn't the only one being left out.

"Enjoying your stay so far?" she asked before turning to the bartender. "Scotch on the rocks."

He nodded and got her the drink.

"Sure. So far, I've seen a prison and the inside of the hotel." I used my cocktail napkin to wipe some condensation from the bar top.

She laughed. "Very exciting. What are you up to now?"

"I'm just killing time. When do you think they'll be done?"

"Why? Looking for Toby?" She gave me a knowing look.

"Maybe." I hid my smile in my drink.

"He's definitely an attractive guy. It's too bad he's unavailable," she mumbled.

"What do you mean?" I moved my straw around the glass.

"He's good at pretending he's over her, but he's not."

"By her you mean Allie?" I sure hoped there wasn't another ex-girlfriend, but hearing he wasn't over anyone didn't feel great.

"Yeah. He's crazy in love with her still."

"Really?" I'm sure there was some iciness in my tone. He'd left me with a very different impression.

"You know what's funny?" She sipped her drink.

"What?"

"The first thing Toby mentioned to me about you was how much you reminded him of Allie."

"You don't say." I pushed away my glass. Suddenly finishing it didn't sound so great.

"Yeah. But I'd take that as a compliment. I mean, you've seen her right? She's gorgeous. Who could compare to that?"

My stomach dropped. "Yeah. Right."

"Oh, honey." She put a hand on my arm. "I'm sorry. You really fell for him, huh?"

I let out a deep breath. "Yeah. I did."

"Toby's never going to settle down. No one can ever live up to Allie."

"You really think he's going to spend his life alone?" I thought about the heartbroken expression on his face every day at the coffee shop. Was he really okay living like that?

"He has work. I think that's enough for him." She took another long drink.

"I guess so."

I forced myself to sit and chat with her a few minutes longer, but I needed some fresh air. After excusing myself, I headed outside and took a walk around the French Quarter. The loud music spilling out of the bars and clubs normally would have lured me in, but not that night. I was frustrated.

It all made sense. Toby hadn't tried anything even when I invited him into my bed. I'd written it off as him being a nice guy, but what if Nelly was right? What if he wasn't over Allie? Was I really going to sit around waiting for a guy again? I'd been hurt that way once before, and I never wanted to experience it again.

I walked around for at least an hour. I stopped at a few tourist shops, but I didn't buy anything. There was something about buying souvenirs on this kind of trip that felt wrong.

I kept thinking about Toby and Allie. I'd caught him looking at her several times over the past few days. I'd given him the benefit of the doubt and assumed it was curiosity, but what if it was more than that? What if he really was still in love with her? Nelly was right about one thing. I couldn't compare to Allie.

After circling around for a while, I made a decision. I wasn't going to make an effort to chase Toby. If he wanted me, he'd let me know. If he wanted to sit around and pine for Allie, I'd let him do it alone. I couldn't blame him completely. I'd known there was something wrong when I first met him. Jess had basically confirmed it, yet I'd pressed on. Sometimes it's easier to turn a blind eye than to face the truth.

I refused to feel sorry for myself as I walked back to the hotel on a mission. I was going to enjoy the rest of my time in New Orleans. Toby and I weren't in a relationship or anything. If I didn't move on, I'd be just as bad as him.

I reached the hotel just in time to see Jared walking out. If there was ever a sign, this was one. Just the sight of him snapped me out of my daze. I followed him when he turned the corner. I had no idea what I was doing, but somehow that didn't matter.

"Where are you going?"

He spun around. "Casey?"

"Where are you going?" I repeated the words.

"Nowhere that concerns you."

"Can I come?" I forced myself to sound confident.

He shook his head. "No."

"Why not?"

"Because it's not safe."

For some reason, I started to cry. Maybe it was just the sting of rejection or a delayed reaction to all the craziness going on. "If it's not safe, why are you going?"

"Are you okay? You're crying."

"Please just ignore it. Can you do that for me?" I didn't want him worried about me. I wanted to have fun. I wanted to stop sitting around and actually live.

A look of concern crossed his face, but then he nodded before continuing like he didn't notice I was desperately trying to hold it together. "Because sometimes you have to take things into your own hands."

"You're going back to Angola." I knew it as plain as day.

"Maybe." His brow furrowed. If we ever played poker, I now knew his tell.

"I'm coming."

"I'm not taking you. It's dangerous and a long flight."

"Flight? You're flying?" I'm sure my eyes were as big as saucers. I'd been thinking about what it would be like to fly with a Pteron since I found out what they were. I needed to get away from the hotel.

"Get that look off your face."

"What look?" I feigned innocence.

"That excited look. I hate that. I don't want to say no to you."

"Then don't. I'll stay out of trouble."

"I don't want to risk getting you hurt."

"Do you want to risk me telling Levi where you're going?" I knew it was low, but I was desperate. I wanted to go with him even though my brain was telling me it was a really bad idea.

"If I take you." He put his hands on my arms. "Will you listen to everything I say?"

"Everything you say?"

"I already told you this is dangerous. I can't have you running off and getting yourself hurt."

I nodded. "I'll listen." What's wrong with you? My brain screamed. Was I willingly going back to that creepy place? But a bigger side of me wanted to go, wanted to do exactly what I wasn't supposed to do. Maybe my teenage rebellion years were coming late.

"Come on." He led me into the shadows in an alley beside the large building and pulled off his shirt.

I bit down the nerves creeping up and let the excitement take over.

"You're going to freeze, but we don't have time for you to change. At least you're in dark colors." He moved behind me, wrapping his arms around my waist.

"I'll be fine. I don't get cold much." I glanced down at my black t-shirt and jeans. Jared's hand settled right around the empty belt loops.

"Try not to scream. I'd prefer to keep my hearing."

We left the ground, and I prepared myself for the fear. It didn't come. Jared's arms remained firmly around me, holding me tightly as he flew.

"Incredible." I wasn't sure if he could hear the words over the wind, but I was saying them for myself as much as him. I felt alive. I felt free.

I kept my eyes wide open, watching the disappearing city lights, and even enjoying the darkness when we reached the country. My heart beat quickly, and my entire body tingled with the energy from being airborne.

So lost in the flight, I was unprepared when Jared landed in a dark corner of the prison yard. Disappointment flooded me. I never wanted the flight to end. Covered in shadows, I could tell he'd picked the spot because it was just outside the reach of the search lights. "Are you okay?"

"Of course. I'm fantastic." I tried to whisper, but my words wanted to come out as a scream. I'd never experienced an adrenaline high like that, only it was more than adrenaline. It was unreal.

"Aren't you cold?"

"Cold? No. Should I be?"

"We were really high up and you're not wearing a jacket." He reached out and touched my bare arms. "Weird. I guess you run warmer than most."

I smiled. "See, you didn't need to worry about me."

"I still need to worry. The hard part is still ahead."

"Maybe I'm really good at sneaking too." I perfected the art in high school when I climbed out my second floor window to see the boyfriend I knew my parents would forbid me to see.

"I guess there's only one way to find out." He tugged on my hand and moved in toward the building.

"We have to get to the north side. A friend's waiting there."

"A friend?"

"Yes, a friend."

"Okay." I let him lead me around the structure.

We stopped in front of a first floor window. "Are you ready for this?"

I nodded.

He stepped through the window, and I followed. The room was pitch black.

"Oh shit." Jared's words echoed across the room.

Someone flipped on the light, and I realized what he'd seen.

"Bryant? How did you get out?" Jared turned to his brother. I couldn't see his face, but I assumed it reflected the same surprise I felt.

"Did you really think I couldn't buy off Derick?" Bryant moved toward Jared, stopping right next to him. He slammed the window shut in the same motion.

This wasn't part of Jared's plan. I had to think quickly. Two large men stood at either side of the interior door, and I was pretty positive that the window wasn't going to open.

"What the hell are you into? Why would you try to take down the Laurents?" Jared asked angrily.

Bryant circled Jared and paused on his other side. "I like to side with the victors, and I knew times were changing."

"Times aren't changing."

"Yes, they are." Bryant laughed. "She's with you again, huh? You brought her back for more?"

"Shut up. She has nothing to do with this."

"You brought her, so she does now." Bryant undressed me with his eyes. I crossed my arms over my chest self-consciously.

"What the hell are you playing at, Bryant?"

"Did you really think I was going to stay locked up like a fucking animal forever?"

Goosebumps covered my body. Whatever was about to happen wouldn't be good.

"So what? You're going to try to kill me? Get rid of your own brother?"

"You had your own brother locked up."

"Because you kidnapped the princess and betrayed the Laurents." Jared's voice rose.

"Wake up. The Laurents aren't perfect. They don't even deserve the crown."

"What's that supposed to mean?" Jared yelled. "More of your vague bull shit?"

"The sad part of all this is that you finally disobeyed Levi and now you're going to pay the price. I guess it's too little too late." Bryant put a hand on Jared's shoulder.

"Pay the price?" Jared sounded nervous for the first time.

One of the guards at the door pulled out a gun and aimed it right at me. Jared lunged toward him. Seconds later, Bryant's hand was on Jared's back right below his wings. He pressed up on the spot where the wings connected to his back.

"Aggh!" Jared let out a harrowing scream.

"It hurts, doesn't it?" Bryant laughed. "Thanks for teaching that little bitch Allie to do it to me. But it's not all that bad. We'll lock you up with some entertainment. I didn't get that." Bryant watched me as he spoke.

Jared stood immobile. Whatever Bryant was doing to Jared's back made it impossible for him to fight back.

"Take over for me," Bryant called to the guard without a gun.

He nodded, strode over, and put his hand where Bryant's was. "Sorry. He paid a lot more than you did, Jared."

I leaned back against the wall. I had to call for help. I hated to even think about him, but Toby was probably the only one I knew of to call. Bryant's attention was back on Jared, so I fished out my phone and had just started to push down Toby's name from the contact list when my phone was ripped from my hand. "And what do you think you're doing?"

"Uh, nothing." I forced myself to look Bryant in the eye. His eyes were so similar to Jared's, but so different. The coldness in his was the exact opposite of the lightness I usually found in Jared's.

"You won't be needing that." He tossed the phone on the floor and stepped on it. When he picked up his shoe, my phone was in pieces. I hoped that the call to Toby had gone through. Bryant grabbed my arms and pulled me tight against his side.

Jared still didn't move, but Bryant positioned me so I had to look right at Jared's face, then he released me. Jared stood there completely immobile with a look of absolute agony on his face. His whole body was in a state of tension.

"Stop that!" I screamed. I couldn't stand seeing him in so much pain.

Bryant laughed a maniacal laugh that made me sick. "What, you don't think he can take it?"

"Stop! Please stop!" I felt the tears. I hated to see him that way.

"Aww, isn't that sweet." Bryant stepped toward me so I stepped backwards until my back became flush against the wall again.

He reached out a hand to touch my cheek, and I slapped it away. "Don't touch me."

He laughed. "Are you really in the position to be telling me what to do?"

"What do you want? You've had your fun, now let us go."

"You're not going anywhere." He grabbed my arm, pulling me down the hall. I screamed for Jared even though I knew he couldn't do anything.

Bryant unlocked a door and towed me down a flight of stairs. We passed rows of cells with bars, but he finally stopped in front of a cell with a door. He used a key to unlock it then pushed me into the dark space. "Enjoy your stay."

A loud thump announced Jared's body landing next to mine just as the door slammed closed behind us.

"Jared!" I knelt down next to him. "Are you okay?"

"I'm fine." He sat up as though nothing had happened. His wings still extended from his back. Long, black, beautiful wings that I wanted to touch. I was losing my mind. I was locked in a cell, and I was thinking about touching a guy's wings.

He moved away from me and over to the door. He pulled on the door, and when that didn't work, he started banging. He must have spent over twenty minutes trying to find a way out. After a while, I couldn't watch. I closed my eyes and tried to pretend I was somewhere else.

***

The light from the bare bulb above us left eerie shadows on the wall. Compared to everything else I'd seen over the past few weeks, it might as well have been bright and cheery holiday decorations. I was getting more and more used to the things that once terrified me.

"Cozy, isn't it?" Jared broke the silence. Despite his tendency to make my blood boil, I was glad to have him with me. The shadows would have bothered me more if I was alone.

"Very. It's hard to believe people don't choose to live here." I paced the tiny cell, needing to burn off some nervous energy in the only way I could.

"On the plus side, we finally have some alone time." He smirked, at least that's what it looked like in the dim lighting.

"It's so romantic."

He laughed. "You can sit down, you know."

"No, thanks."

"There's plenty of room over here." He patted a spot on the cot next to him. Somehow, his attempt to break the door had ended with him sitting peacefully. I didn't see that change of demeanor coming.

"I'm okay over here." I paused my pacing in front of the door. "I wouldn't want to miss my chance to escape."

"To escape this cell or me?"

"Aren't they one and the same?"

He smiled. "Escaping me is going to be hard even outside."

"I didn't know you were into the whole chase thing. I'd have pegged you for a wait for the girl to come to you kind of guy."

I don't know why I was playing into his game. I guess I saw it as the distraction he was offering. That explained the calm. He was trying to make sure I didn't freak out. I appreciated the effort even if I wasn't telling him that.

"Usually I am."

"But this time is different?" I rested the heel of my boot against the door.

"Yeah. Isn't it obvious? I went through a lot of effort to get us locked in here."

"Oh, so this was intentional?"

"You didn't think I'd actually let myself get locked in a cell, did you?"

I laughed. "Never. You're too strong for that."

"Glad you noticed."

"Do you think anyone else is around? Is there anyone who can help?"

"Let's find out." He stood up, giving me another peek at his shirtless body. These Pterons had ruined me for other guys. I couldn't imagine how many hours at a gym it would take a human to get a physique like that.

"How?"

"Hello? Anyone around?" Jared screamed.

"Stop that!" I hissed. "What if someone comes?"

"Isn't that what we want?" A smile tugged at his lips. "Unless you like being locked in here with me."

Ugh. I didn't even bother to reply. "Help!"

No one answered.

"I guess we know we're alone."

"Great."

"We'll get out. You just have to time it right." He took a single step toward me.

"Time it right?" I watched him. Did he have an escape plan up his sleeve?

"If we tried to escape now, they'd be waiting. We have to act when they think we've given up."

"That's why you haven't broken us out yet?"

"Of course. What did you think?" He crossed the small space and stopped next to me.

"I think I want to go home."

"I want to take you home." He leaned back against the wall.

"To your place, or mine?"

"Depends. What's your bed like?"

"A twin in my cousin's closet."

"Then mine. It's much better than that." There was a promise in his words, and it went beyond a nice mattress and sheets.

"It's not hard to beat." I leaned back next to him.

"Is there a story behind the living arrangement? Couldn't afford to rent his bathroom or something?"

"Yeah, I prefer a bed to the tub, and I even get to use the shower."

"Generous landlord."

"Very. He gives me a family discount." Joking felt good. For a second, I almost forgot where we were.

"Wow. That's even better. And if you live in a closet, that means you can get dressed faster in the morning."

"My clothes are in the living room."

"It's *that* small of a closet?" he asked incredulously.

"It fits my bed."

"Do you at least have a door?" He turned his head to look at me.

"I do!" I clapped my hands as though I was sharing the most exciting reality ever. "And it even has a lock!"

He laughed. "Awesome. If you have a lock, it might be doable."

"Oh yeah? You'd slum it in a closet as long as it has a lock?"

"For you? Yeah."

I leaned my head back. "Do you live in a penthouse, too?"

"No. I live in a shotgun style house a few blocks from campus. I'm moving out to my own place soon though."

"Are you planning to stay in New Orleans?"

"Why?" He reached his hand over and brushed his fingers over mine in a surprisingly gentle caress. "Worried you won't get to see me enough?"

"Just curious. I mean, if we're going to be locked in a cell together, I might as well learn more about you."

"More about me, huh? Are you sure you don't want to sit down for this?"

"You're all about getting me on a bed with you, huh?"

"I'm okay with this wall too, but I'm a little worried about your back."

"Glad to know you're concerned."

"I'm very concerned with your well-being." He scooted closer.

"Oh yeah? I didn't know you were the caring type."

"You've made a lot of judgments about me." He moved in front of me, his hips stopping only inches from mine.

"And you haven't made any judgments about me?"

"Only ones I know are true."

"Is that so?" I knew I sounded flirtatious, and I couldn't help it.

"Yeah."

"What are they?"

"You like to pretend you're a good girl, but you're not."

I cough-choked. "Where'd you get that idea?"

"I can just tell. Like right now, the way you're responding to me. You like how close I am, but if we were in broad daylight, you'd be pushing me away."

"I'm not pushing you away now."

"No. You're not." His eyes locked with mine, and it was like he could see right into my mind.

"Is this how you usually pick up your prey?"

"My prey?" He smiled. "I don't generally consider women to be prey."

"You don't?"

"First you say I don't chase, and now you say I view girls as prey. Which one is it?"

"A hunter doesn't always run after his mark. Sometimes he sits and waits."

"Oh yeah? So now you're telling me I set traps?"

"You do. You know how to lure girls in, and you know exactly the moment when there's no turning back."

"Are you in that moment now?" He leaned close to me, half an inch more and our faces would have been touching.

"No." I touched the wall behind me, needing to remind myself of where and what I was doing.

"That's too bad." His lips skimmed mine.

"Why is it too bad?" A shiver ran through me.

"Because I was thinking we could make the best of the situation."

"You can stop trying to distract me." I needed him to stop before I did something stupid. But for some reason, letting Jared kiss me didn't seem like a mistake—it seemed perfect.

"Distract you? Who said I was trying to distract you?"

"Me."

"I'd do a much better job if I was trying to distract you."

"Yeah?"

"Want to see?"

I nodded. My head told me not to, but my body said something else entirely.

He brushed his lips against mine again. I thought maybe he was all talk, but then he ran his teeth over my bottom lip. "I promise to make you forget where you are." His lips moved against mine, first slow, then faster and faster until he lightly bit down.

I moaned and let go of the wall so I could wrap my arms around him. He pushed into my mouth while one of his hands slipped underneath my shirt and bra all in one movement. He squeezed my breast, and I pushed my body against his.

The kiss deepened further and further until I was dizzy. His hand left my breast, and I missed the touch immediately. I groaned.

He laughed, stepping back from me. "Remember where you are, Casey?"

It took me a second to respond. "I didn't, but I do now."

"You shouldn't have said that."

Before I could reply, he had me pinned against the wall with his arms on either side of me. His lips were on mine again, and I eagerly welcomed him back. He tasted so damn good, the opposite of the dank room we were trapped in. I wanted more. I wanted all of him.

His hand moved to the button of my jeans, and I didn't stop him. Nothing else mattered. Not the fact that we were locked in a cell in a part of the prison that didn't technically exist or that I barely knew him. He slipped his hand into my jeans, brushing his fingers over my panties, but then he pulled his hand out and stopped kissing me.

He smiled. "You test my resistance."

"I do?" I struggled to pull out of my fog. Damn that guy could kiss.

He laughed. "Yes. We need to get out of here."

"And you know how we're going to do that?" I buttoned my jeans.

"Yes, but first, what's your number?"

"Excuse me?"

"Tell me your phone number."

"You're asking me for my phone number at a time like this?"

"Considering how close I got to taking you against a cell wall, you shouldn't be too surprised."

I shivered at his words. They sounded better than I'd ever admit out loud. "631-555-0120"

"631-555-0120." He repeated the numbers back.

"You memorized it already?"

"I've got a good memory. Now let's get out of here."

"How?"

He smirked. "Just give it two minutes."

I heard the grunts first and then the door was wrenched open.

"Casey?" Toby sounded panicked as he ran into the cell with Owen.

"Yeah, I'm here." I looked at him guiltily. I reminded myself about what Nelly said. He'd never get over Allie.

He hugged me, making the guilt even worse. I pulled away so we could walk out.

Jared tugged on my arm, pulling me further from Toby as we headed down the corridor. We didn't pass any guards that were upright, but there were quite a few on the ground.

"When we get out of here, you'll have to explain to me how the hell you managed to get locked up in a cell." Owen laughed as we slid through the same window we'd entered from.

"How much trouble am I in?" Jared looked nervous for the first time that night. He hadn't even seemed nervous when he discovered he couldn't break us out.

"Tons."

"Fantastic. I guess this means I'm going to have to cancel on our plans, Casey." He let out an exaggerated sigh.

"What plans?" I asked.

"It's way past eight, but I was supposed to take you out tonight."

"You kind of did. Just not downtown." After the words came out, I realized how bad they sounded. As disappointed as I was about how things went down with Toby, I didn't want to hurt him.

"He's going to kill you." Owen brought the conversation back to Levi.

"Yeah, well. At least if I die, I had a good time tonight."

"A good time?" Owen asked and then looked at me. "I know girls can't resist him, but in a prison cell?"

"I didn't have sex with him!"

Jared laughed. "No, you guys arrived too soon."

Toby growled. Even more than his wings, the growl made him seem less human. I needed to get back to New York and away from the whole mess.

I turned back to Toby. "Can I take your plane home?"

"You want to leave tonight?"

"I need to."

He nodded. "Then we will."

I wasn't looking forward to spending time on a plane with him, but I couldn't wait to get back in my little bed in the closet.

Chapter Twenty-Five

Jared

Avoiding Levi would only make things worse. The more time I gave him to stew over things, the angrier he'd be. I needed to hit it head on.

He was waiting for me on his front porch. Either he'd been listening or he knew I'd come over to face his wrath. In all my years of knowing Levi, I'd never crossed him that way. I'd also never gotten myself into such a ridiculously dumb situation.

"I assume you have an explanation." He sat in an Adirondack chair, giving me a look that was half annoyance and half pity. I could handle the annoyance but not the pity.

"I couldn't let it go."

"Obviously. Why I didn't plan on you being such an idiot, I'll never know."

"It's not my fault he broke out."

"I never said it was."

"Then what are you angry about?" I leaned back against one of the columns, just waiting for him to stand up and confront me face to face.

"You deliberately disobeyed me, and you put an innocent human at risk."

"Disobeyed? What am I your puppy now?" I took a seat on the railing.

"I've put up with your crap for years, but I am your superior. It would be nice if you showed an ounce of respect once in a while."

"You're my superior because you were born into it." I'd never voiced those words before, and I instantly regretted them.

"Are you implying I don't deserve to be king?" He finally stood up and moved toward me.

"No. But I am saying you don't know everything."

"And you do? You know the best way to handle things, huh?"

"Maybe I was too late, but waiting longer wouldn't have helped either. The bottom line is Bryant escaped. Now what?"

"Now I decide what the hell to do with you." He looked toward the front door then back at me. Maybe he was afraid Allie was listening in. She probably was.

"Are you threatening to fire me?"

"I should fire you. That would be the responsible thing to do."

"You've never been responsible, Levi."

He cracked a smile. "Not often. That's why I'm giving you another chance to prove yourself."

"How?"

"Find Bryant. Find out who's behind these attacks. I'll give you whatever tools you need."

"I won't let you down."

"I know you won't, but I'll be watching."

"I need to go back to New York. That's where it started so that's where I need to be."

"And this has nothing to do with that girl?" He raised an eyebrow.

"No." That was mostly true.

"Don't screw this up. I'm not giving you another chance."

"I get that."

"All right, can you guys just hug and make up. It's getting late." Allie graced us with her presence, walking out on the porch in a Tulane hoodie and shorts.

Levi turned to her. "You really need to do a better job eavesdropping."

"Why? You didn't make me leave." She grinned.

"All right, I'll leave you guys to whatever it is you'd be doing if I wasn't here." I gave a wave and nodded to Levi as I left the porch.

"Don't let me down, Jared. I don't want to lose you."

"I won't." I meant it.

Two days later, I was packed and ready to go. Owen gave me a ride to the airport. As convenient as flying myself can be, it's more difficult when you're trying to bring a couple pieces of luggage with you.

"Do you think you'll be back for graduation?" He pulled over to the curb outside departures.

"Maybe. I don't really care whether I walk." Luckily, I didn't need to finish any of my classes to graduate. I had enough credits by the end of my junior year. There just never seemed to be any rush to finish.

"If you get bored again, just give me a call."

"I won't get bored."

He grinned. "Tell her I said hi."

"Who says I'm talking about Casey?"

"You just did." He lightly punched my arm.

"I don't know if I'll even call her."

"You know she dumped Toby."

"What?" Was he serious?

"Yeah. Hailey and Allie were talking about it."

Had Casey dumped Toby for me? Maybe what happened in the cell meant more to her than I thought.

I checked-in for my flight and called Allie. My curiosity had gotten the best of me.

"Missing me already?" Allie didn't bother with a normal greeting.

I let out a deep breath. Allie was never going to let me hear the end of this. "I heard Casey broke it off with Toby."

"You heard right. But the question is who told you?"

"Owen."

"Oh, I guess he heard me telling Hailey."

"When did it happen?"

"Right after she got back to New York. She's feeling pretty awful about it, but she didn't want to lead him on I guess."

"Wait. You talked to her?"

"How else would I know?"

"Why were you talking to Casey?" I wasn't sure how I felt about Allie and Casey having some sort of friendship.

"I was worried about her. I happen to know how frustrating the Pteron world can be to humans."

"Sure, sure. Did she mention me?"

"Oh my god. I wish I could record this conversation. Yes, she mentioned you. Call her."

"I might."

"She really likes you."

"You think?"

"I know. And now you're scaring me. You never get weird about girls."

"I'm not being weird."

"Don't use her, Jared. I like her."

"Good to know." I reached my gate. "I've got to go. Talk to you soon." I hung up, ready to get to New York.

***

"Hello?" That sweet yet sultry voice answered the phone, and I knew I'd made the right decision. I'd debated whether to call her or not for weeks, but I could still picture how good that body of hers felt against mine, and my willpower lost out. Girls didn't usually do that to me. I liked them, but I didn't need them. At least not anyone in particular. Casey was different. She'd gotten under my skin, and our few stolen moments in that prison cell weren't going to cut it. I needed to finish what I'd started. Maybe then I'd get her out of my head. Besides, she'd dumped Toby for me. I'd be an ass if I didn't at least go see her.

"Hello there. I'm looking for a girl I used to share a cell with. Any idea where I can find her?"

"Jared?" She sounded both surprised and excited. "I wondered if I'd ever hear from you."

"Did you? Glad to know you've been thinking about me." I leaned back against a brick wall.

"You left an impression. Believe it or not, you're the only guy I've ever made out with while trapped in a prison."

"Yeah? Glad I can be your first in one way." I was glad I'd given her one memorable night. If things went my way, I'd be giving her an even more memorable one.

"How are things in New Orleans?"

"I wouldn't know."

"Why not?"

"Look outside your balcony window." I watched as that pretty face of hers peeked out.

"I don't see anything."

I stepped out of the shadows, and she jumped back from the glass door.

"Jared?" she asked with disbelief when she opened the door.

"I thought I'd come by for a visit."

"I'm glad." She was wearing a little set of PJs. They showed off her legs and just enough cleavage to make my pants tight.

"Do you want to come in?" She sounded coy, but the look in her eyes could only be read one way. She wanted me as much as I wanted her.

"I thought I'd take you for a flight."

"A flight, huh?"

"Sound good?" I watched her, assuming she knew I was talking about two different kinds of flights.

"Yeah. I should change though."

"Don't." I reached out for her arm and pulled her against me. "I'm the only one who's going to be looking at you, and you'll be wearing less than that very soon."

"Will I?" She smiled at me in a teasing way.

"Yes, you will. I hope you know what you're getting into though." I closed the balcony door. She wasn't going back inside that night.

"And what's that?"

"A night you'll never forget."

I tightened my hold on her and jumped off the balcony. Her chest was pressed against mine, and she was staring up while we flew. By the look of euphoria on her face, she liked it.

I landed on my balcony without releasing her. We were on the highest floor, so I wasn't worried about too many people seeing us.

I laid her on the padded double chaise and pressed my weight down on her. I wasn't messing around. "I've missed you, Casey, and it's time to find out just how much you've missed me."

"Oh yeah?" Her eyes were wide with anticipation and adrenaline from the flight.

"Yeah." I pulled her shirt over her head, refusing to have any fabric separating our chests. I needed her skin against mine, and I needed my mouth on her. I tasted the first breast while fondling the other, all the while keeping my eyes trained on hers. I wasn't going to miss a second of her reaction. She reached out to fumble with my belt buckle and finally released me from the jeans I'd been straining against.

Her hands were tentative, but mine weren't as I pushed down her shorts and panties in one motion. Without moving my mouth from her breast, I spread open her legs with my free hand.

She moaned, her hand tightening around me.

I shifted out of my jeans, kicking them, along with my boxers, off the chair.

I had her completely naked and waiting for me, looking up at me with an expression of anticipation and nerves that was so completely hot it actually tested my resistance.

She felt so good, so wet, hot and ready. I took her lips, wanting her moans against my mouth. She squirmed under me and that only made me want to make her do it more.

She stroked me, and I wasn't sure how much more I could take. I unwrapped one of the condoms I'd stuffed into my jeans.

I spread her legs wider, slipping between her thighs the way I'd wanted to for weeks.

"Jared, please."

Those two words nearly undid me, and I thrust into her. She was tight and wet. Perfect. I grabbed her ass as she wrapped her legs around me. I pushed into her over and over, loving that each time she reacted more, her breathing becoming heavier and her nails digging into my back. I could have taken it easy on her, but I didn't want to. I wasn't going to be satisfied until I'd used up every ounce of her strength. Her gasps and screams of passion eventually pushed me over the edge. I released, feeling a level of satisfaction sex had stopped giving me years ago.

Sweaty and out of breath, she lay there watching me. "Oh my god."

I kissed her, something I never did after sex. Her lips were still sweet, but also salty now.

"I'm not sure I ever want to let you go."

"You don't have to yet."

"No. I don't." I picked her up, leaving our clothes behind as I opened the French door, never putting her down even as I walked us to the bathroom and turned on the water. I needed her wet, surrounded in steam. I needed her like we hadn't just fucked so hard I could still feel her tightness around me.

I pushed her up against the wall, glad to see the eagerness in her eyes. "Do you want more, Casey?"

"Yes."

"How much more?" I needed to push her, to see if she was as affected by our physical connection as I was.

"Lots."

"When do you want more?"

"Now."

She got what she asked for. She screamed louder this time. Maybe it's because we weren't outside or maybe it was the echo in the bathroom, but it's like her cries surrounded me. I could feel them. We moved together so damn well, like our bodies were designed to be locked together in a constant stream of motion. Her legs wrapped around me so tight I could barely stand up. I just pushed her back harder against the wall and thrust deeper. I wanted her to feel every inch of me.

"Jared." She called my name before biting into my shoulder. I did the same to her as I released. I'd never bitten a girl, but I was out of control.

That should have been enough. That should have led to us sprawled out together in my bed, fast asleep, but it was only the beginning. I couldn't stop and neither could she. We were like animals, needy and desperate, and unable or unwilling to come up for air. The sun was already half up by the time her eyes closed. We were back in my bed, the sheets tousled and tangled at our feet.

Moments later, her breathing evened out, and I realized she'd fallen asleep. I still felt like I was inside of her. I'd lost track of how many times we'd gone, and I just hoped that wasn't it. It couldn't be. I'd finally met my match in a girl, and there wasn't a chance in hell I was letting her go.

Chapter Twenty-Six

Casey

My entire body ached. Every inch of me pulsed and buzzed with Jared. I could feel him, smell him, taste him everywhere. His arms and legs covered me like a blanket as we lay there completely exposed in the middle of his bed. What the hell had happened to us the night before? I'd dreamed about having sex with him, but it was nothing like that. Not that mind blowing experience that I couldn't possibly explain in words. We'd spent hours tangled up in each other. We'd moved together in so many different ways, but each had been fantastic, exciting, and new in its own right. I ran a hand down his muscular back. My fingers moved slowly over a bite mark on his shoulder. Had I actually bitten him?

"Morning, babe," he mumbled against my neck.

"I think it's afternoon." The sun was high in the sky, and it was the heat and light pouring through the window that woke me up.

"Same difference." He nipped at my neck and squeezed one of my breasts.

"That was some night."

"Absolutely fucking amazing."

"I don't know what got into me." My sexual experience was limited, and I'd always been a fairly timid partner. My performance the night before had been anything but timid.

"Sure you do, Casey. I got into you." His hand slid down my body, stopping on my inner thigh.

"Yes. Yes, you did."

"How are you feeling?" He made tiny circles on the sensitive skin of my thigh.

"Not ready for more."

He laughed. "Did I really tire you out that much?"

"Yes."

"Are you sure?" His fingers moved slightly. "I can be very, very gentle."

"Can you?"

"Yes."

"Interesting."

"Just for that, you'll have to let me show you."

"How about you show me another time? That is if there's another time." I wanted there to be another time. I wanted whatever earth shaking experience we'd shared to be more than a little fling. I wanted to think there was a possibility of something real. I wasn't going to accept that it was a night of meaningless sex. I was meant to be with a Pteron—I was meant to be with Jared.

"There will be." A look of surprise crossed his face, like he couldn't believe he was saying it.

"I take it your answer is usually no."

"Usually, but not today. I have to have you again."

"You will."

"But not now?" He kissed one of my breasts.

"Not now." I was too full of emotion and too sore to contemplate it.

"Want me to get your clothes?"

"We left them outside, didn't we?"

"Yeah…we didn't exactly need them again last night." He grinned.

"It's not like I can go home in my pajamas. Do you happen to have something for me to wear?"

"I have a better idea."

"What's that?"

"Let me make you something to eat, hang out here, and I'll fly you home when it gets dark."

"Can we sleep a little longer?"

"Absolutely." He adjusted us so my head was leaning on his chest. "I'm pretty comfortable."

"Me too."

Chapter Twenty-Seven

Toby

Things would work out. They needed to. Casey hadn't given me much of a reason for why she suddenly pulled back, but I had my suspicions. His name was Jared.

I'd heard he was back in New York, but thankfully he hadn't showed up in my office. I hoped he wasn't back just for her. I could make myself swallow the thought of her wanting a fling with Jared, but the thought of them developing a relationship longer than that hurt like hell. I refused to accept it.

Luckily, the attacks had died down, but it felt more like the calm before the storm than any real resolution. Both Murphy and Bryant had disappeared without a trace.

I'd opened myself up to Casey just to have the door slammed in my face. I probably should have moved on, but I couldn't. Everything reminded me of her, even coffee. I refused to make it easy on her. I'd give her space because she seemed to want it, but I wasn't giving up. I showed up at Coffee Heaven every day.

"You want your usual?" She smiled at me, but it wasn't the kind of smile I was looking for. She was back to pretending I was just one of her customers.

"No. I'll have something different today."

"Oh?"

"A double espresso."

"Coming right up." She turned around, and I felt a sense of loss. I missed looking at her face.

She set the espresso down on the counter. "Are you doing all right?"

"Yeah. Missing you though."

A sad expression crossed her face. "It's not me you're missing."

"What's that supposed to mean?" I picked up my cup.

"Never mind." She moved on to help another customer.

I was still thinking about our conversation when I sat mindlessly flipping through the channels on the TV later that night. The only logical explanation was that she thought I was still into Allie. How could she possibly believe that after the time we'd spent together? We might not have had sex, but there was something special about the night we spent in New Orleans. I only wished she'd felt it too.

My phone rang, and I picked up half expecting it to be her. I missed her voice. "Hello?"

"It's Cody. Someone dropped off something for you. Should I bring it up?"

"What is it?"

"Just some manila envelope with your name on it." Cody was never very forthcoming with details.

"And who brought it?"

"The bear who works with Casey. I think his name is Eric."

"Send it up." I hung up and headed to the door. It wouldn't take Cody long.

I heard him before he knocked so I opened the door. Cody handed over the envelope before turning and stepping back into the elevator.

I sat down on the sofa and tore open the flap. Inside, I found two sheets of off-white paper. The first one was a handwritten note addressed to me.

Toby-

I thought it was time you learned the truth. I can't protect her on my own, and I thought this might help shed some light.

-Eric

Unsure of what to expect on the next sheet, I glanced at it.

The red text on the top had my attention immediately: Confidential-Paternity Results

"Paternity results?" What the hell did this have to do with anything?

The name on the next line didn't surprise me, but it still made my chest clench. Casey Morgan Bates.

I scanned over several paragraphs about authorizations and where the test was administered before I finally looked at the bottom of the paper. Robert Laurent. The name froze me in place. Her father was Robert Laurent? Shit. Casey was Levi's sister?

Chapter Twenty-Eight

Casey

Jared didn't fly me home until after ten o'clock. Neither of us were in a particularly big rush to say goodnight, but a phone call from Levi snapped us back to reality. Jared had work to do, and I needed sleep.

An hour later, I stood under the lukewarm spray of my shower, thinking back on an entirely different shower experience from the night before. Usually I kept my showers short, because even the mildly warm water would turn cold, but getting out of the shower meant moving on from the single most incredible twenty-four hours of my life.

When the water neared the icy level, I stopped fighting the inevitable. I shut it off and reached out for a towel.

I thought I heard a noise outside the door. "Jared?" I called, hoping he'd finished his work and had come by to visit. The thought of anyone else being in my apartment sent shivers through my body.

No one answered. I pulled on my clothes, glad I'd brought them into the bathroom with me. I was used to living with a male roommate.

I opened the door carefully. "Hello?"

Once again, no answer. The hair on the back of my neck stood up. Something was off.

I tiptoed down the hall to my room.

"Hello, Casey." Two strong arms grabbed me from behind.

My heart dropped as soon as I heard Murphy's voice.

After a moment, I regained the capacity for speech. "What are you doing here?"

"Tonight seemed like a good night to give you a little lesson." He put a cloth over my mouth, never letting go of my arms. I struggled, but it did nothing. I was so tired of feeling weak around these paranormal creatures. He easily bound my arms together.

Murphy pulled me from my apartment and dragged me down the stairs. I tried to scream, but for the second time in a month, a gag prevented me from getting a sound out. I hoped someone would randomly come out of their apartment, but no one did. Moments later, Murphy shoved me into the backseat of an unmarked car.

The drive seemed endless, but it was probably only ten minutes. As soon as the car stopped, Murphy pulled me out and dragged me to a service entrance of the Empire State Building. If I had use of my hands, I would have pinched myself to make sure I wasn't dreaming. The nightmarish experience needed to end.

He inserted a key in the elevator and we shot up to the 102nd floor. From there, he dragged me up another two sets of stairs before opening a door to the outside. We were on the roof.

He untied my hands and ungagged me. "Have a nice trip?"

"What are we doing here?" I wanted to scream and fight, but staying calm seemed like the best plan. I had to find a way to get past him and back to the stairs.

"You'll see."

"That's not good enough. You kidnap me and drag me to the Empire State Building in the middle of the night, and you tell me I'll see?"

He laughed. "You're always asking questions, Casey. How about you find your own answers for once?"

"I wish I could find them. Maybe if you told me where Vera was, I'd get some."

"All in good time."

"Come on. Why are we here? Do you want to kill me?" We were on the roof of the tallest building in the city.

"If I wanted you dead, it would have happened a long time ago. I want the opposite."

"You're not making any sense." Wind burned my face. All I wanted to do was go home and crawl back into my bed…or Jared's.

"I am. If you'd only think about it." He stepped closer to me, making me move away from the wall.

"I am thinking. I think you're a jerk and a bully. I think it's time to leave me the hell alone."

He laughed again. "I'm not your enemy. I'm trying to be your friend here. What I do for you tonight will be the greatest gift you've ever received."

"I don't want anything from you but my sister."

"It's time for you to find out who you really are." Murphy had me cornered. If I stepped back any further, I'd be a pancake on the street below.

"Who I really am? I know who I am."

"Do you? Do you know who your parents are?"

"Yes. Tami and Chris Bates."

He laughed. It was a laugh laced with anger and it chilled me. "Chris isn't your father."

"Uh, yes he is."

"No he's not."

I shook my head. None of this made sense.

"It's true. Vera is only your half-sister, by the way."

"I don't believe you."

"She misses you."

"I'm not going to believe a word you say." I couldn't, it was too much to take in. "Chris is my father."

"Deluding yourself isn't going to change the fact that your father is a much more powerful man."

"I don't believe you." I started to shake.

"You met your half-brother recently. He's a real piece of work."

"I don't have a half-brother. Just like Vera isn't my half-sister."

"Yes, you do. He doesn't know about you yet."

"Who is it?" I didn't really believe a word he was saying, but part of me was afraid that there could be some truth in it.

"I'll give you one clue."

"What's that?"

"He's the king."

"Levi? You're telling me Levi and I are related?"

"Uh huh. Think about that, sweetheart."

"No. Just stop messing with me!" My body shook again. I wanted to lunge at him, but that would only lead to me getting hurt.

"Are you getting angry, Casey? Do you feel out of control?"

I shook my head.

"I told you it was time to find out who you really are."

"What are you talking about?"

"Take off your sweater."

"No way."

"Take off your sweater."

"No!"

He closed the distance between us, ripping off my sweater and leaving me in just a tank top.

"What, my sister isn't enough for you? Now you're going after me?"

"I don't want you for that, Casey. Vera's more than enough for me. Sorry to disappoint you."

"What do you want from me?" I struggled to maintain my balance.

"I already told you what I want right now."

"For me to figure out who I am?" I wrapped my arms around myself tighter.

"Exactly." He stepped toward me once more. "I really hope you figure it out fast." A grin crossed his lips. "Have a nice time. Let me know how it is for you."

"What?"

"Do you know how high up we are?"

"No."

"We're at nearly fifteen hundred feet and you have less than ten seconds to figure it out." He pushed me.

I lost my footing and had no time to react. My body was launched off the building. The world flew by as I fell freely through the air. I should have been scared, I should have been crying, but instead my body got warm. I felt a sensation I'd never felt before, and a searing pain spread throughout my entire body.

Suddenly, I wasn't falling anymore. I leveled out, and my heart returned to its normal speed. I glanced back, wondering who had caught me, but I only saw black wings. The truth set in. No one caught me, I'd caught myself. The wings were mine.

The wings moved without me consciously thinking about them. I headed away from the city street, up above the buildings and higher. I laughed. I laughed harder than I ever had before. All these years, I'd had the potential for this? To escape everything? To leave the ground behind? After constantly falling, it was time to soar.

If you missed the beginning of the Pteron story, be sure to check out ***Flight*, Book 1 of the Crescent Chronicles**!

www.AlyssaRoseIvy.com
www.facebook.com/AlyssaRoseIvy
twitter.com/AlyssaRoseIvy
AlyssaRoseIvy@gmail.com

To stay up to date on Alyssa's new releases, join her mailing list: http://eepurl.com/ktlSj

Printed in Great Britain
by Amazon.co.uk, Ltd.,
Marston Gate.